F

Slim Returns

Marina Johnson

Tamarillas Press

This book is a work of fiction. All characters, locations, businesses, organisations and situations in this publication are either a product of the author's imagination or used fictitiously. Any resemblance to real persons, living or dead, is purely coincidental.

ISBN: 9781708388997

Other books by Marina Johnson

Fat Girl Slim
Fat Girl Slim Three
Say Hello and Wave Goodbye
So Talk To Me
A Confusion of Murders
The Harriet Way
The Herb Sisters

Writing as Joanne Ryan
Without Reason
All The Lost Years
The Double
The Lodger
One Night
Lie To Me
Not Your Average Girl

CHAPTER ONE

I watch from the side of the stage as Doris stands proudly next to the life size cardboard cut-out of me at my fattest. The picture of me in my Foodco leggings and humungous red t-shirt dwarfs Doris, making her seem even daintier than she is. She looks like a pretty little fairy with the bright stage lights picking out the expensive platinum highlights in her perfectly styled hair. Her cute pink dress with matching pink towering heels completes the look and suits her petite frame perfectly.

I run through my speech in my head while I wait to make my entrance. I've practised it so often that as soon as I say the first sentence the rest of it flows quite naturally. I just have to remember not to stand too close to the cut-out of me when I go onto the stage because Aiden has warned me that if I do it'll make it obvious that the cut-out has been enlarged. A good head higher than the real me it's been blown up to make the old me appear even fatter than I really was.

As if the old me wasn't fat enough already.

'I'm thrilled to announce that the author of the ground-breaking non-diet eating plan, *The Travis Way*, will be with us very shortly. Frogham's very own Alison Travis has just finished giving an exclusive interview on the BBC Breakfast show and is en-route to us at this very moment.'

As Doris finishes speaking she steps neatly to one side of the stage and raises her arm and points her hand at the drop down screen behind her.

'While we wait for her, let's just remind ourselves why we're all here today.' As if by magic the screen fills with a huge image of my already best-selling book, *The Travis Way*. The cover shows the slim me superimposed over the old inflated fat me to show just how much weight has been lost. The basics of the *non-diet diet* are relayed to the audience by a deep voiced man in a commanding and convincing manner whilst images of my former fat self looking thoroughly downtrodden and miserable are flashed onto the screen. These are interspersed with images of the new me looking glamorous and slim in various colourful gym wear and expensive designer clothing. I'm pretty sure they've digitally altered the expression on my face on the fat picture to make me look miserable because I distinctly remember feeling optimistic at the time I took the photo; I'm sure I was smiling.

I'm also quite certain that I only ever took one

photograph of myself even though there appear to be lots of pictures of fat me wearing different clothing – the wonders of digital manipulation I assume. I'd never intended to take a *before* picture of myself because I hated myself so much that I didn't need reminding of how I fat I was; I could hardly bear to look in the mirror let alone take selfies. I also knew that I'd attempted so many diets in the past that I'd probably end up fatter than when I'd started and I didn't need a photograph of myself to remind me of my failure.

I'd changed my mind about a *before* picture after only one week of dieting and thumping around the lounge to try and get fitter because I'd lost an astonishing eight pounds – but, more importantly, I was feeling optimistic and confident and starting to think that maybe I *could* lose weight after all. I look at the photo of the old me now and I barely recognise myself, I'm not that person anymore – either mentally or physically.

I peer around the edge of the curtain and scan the room to see how many people are here and I have to admit that it's an impressive audience. Every single one of the red flock covered seats in the theatre has a bum on it and there is also a throng of people standing along the back of the aisles watching the stage. A sell out – although it was actually free to get in because Aiden said that the book sales would cover the hire charge and make a tidy profit as well.

The audiences' attention is fixed firmly on the

screen as the deep voiced man continues to intone the benefits of *The Travis Way.* I only have a close-up view of the first few rows and I can see that unsurprisingly the majority of them are either fat or on the chubby side.

Out in the floral carpeted foyer, Aiden has arranged for a signing station to be set up which consists of two tables with copies of my book piled high. The tables are positioned next to a desk where I can sit and autograph the books after the presentation - *after* people have paid fourteen pounds ninety-nine to buy them, of course.

This is only the second occasion that I've ever been inside Frogham Theatre despite living here for my entire life. The only other occasion was when I came here on a school trip to watch *Hamlet* when I was twelve and although I don't remember anything about the play, I do remember being very excited to be here because apart from attending school I never went anywhere. The theatre has lots of visiting shows and artists and they put on a pantomime every Christmas – when I was a child every year I used to beg Mother to bring me but she never would, of course. Mother had no time for the theatre and said it was run by poofs and adulterers – her words, not mine.

Aiden, the marketing expert who's planned the publicity campaign for *The Travis Way,* thought that my home town would be the perfect place to kick off the publicity tour before taking it around the rest of the country but events have rather over taken us. The book is already on the best seller list which is mostly due to the ads on Instagram that Aiden organised which for some reason caught fire and jettisoned my book into the bestseller ranks. Aiden didn't think the ads would do very much at all and said that they were relatively cheap to do so thought he'd give them a try, but something about *The Travis Way* caught the public's imagination and it's been flying off the shelves. Aiden thinks it might have something to do with the unseasonal heat wave that we're enjoying even though it's only March; his theory is that people are starting their diets for the summer earlier than usual. I think he's right; everyone has suddenly realised that they need to get the blubber off before the hell of bikini season arrives.

You would think that the audience would be sick of the film by now because I've seen it twice myself since I arrived and I'm sure it was played several times before I even got here.

According to Aiden the first rule of marketing is that you have to keep people waiting, keep them wanting; the more you withhold something, the more people want it and while they're waiting you bombard them with images of what you want them to buy to make them want it even more. The more times they see the film, the more likely they are to buy the book. Like brain washing, I remarked to Aiden, but I don't think he liked it because he sighed and pursed his lips and said it was definitely *not* brain washing but was more about persuading people who didn't know that they wanted my book that they did want it and absolutely *must* have it.

So. Brain washing, then.

While the film is running Doris slips off the stage to join me in the wings.

'Good turnout, init?' She whispers as she slips her feet out of her shoes and wiggles and stretches her toes, wincing as she does so.

I smile and nod. Doris – or Doe, as she now calls herself professionally – has been a revelation. When on stage, or *on duty* as she calls it, she ditches the chav speak and adopts a semi posh accent. I'd say it's *sort* of a transatlantic drawl but a lot of people take her for an Australian because it's a difficult accent to pin down. But it's definitely not chav; no dropped aitches and no swearing either. I think it takes a huge amount of effort on her part because as soon as she's out of anyone else's earshot she's back to her old self. It's a kind of acting, Doris tells me.

I've got to be honest, I didn't think she had it in her to be a presenter and when I offered her a job I was thinking more along the lines of humping boxes of books around and maybe a spot of shoving leaflets through letter boxes. I felt I owed her because she'd always been a good friend to me so when she got sacked from Moppers the very least I could do was offer her a job.

I never did get to the bottom of why she got the sack; she was very vague about the reasons and when pressed said it was something to do with using the wrong colour cleaning cloth but I'm sure there was more to it than that. Anyway, she talked me into letting her have a go at doing a sales pitch to Aiden so I thought, well, where's the harm - she'll embarrass herself and that'll be that and I'll give her a few boxes of leaflets to post around Frogham and then pay her far more than the going rate because it's not like I can't afford it.

Only it didn't turn out quite like that; the first shock was when she arrived at Aiden's office to do her pitch. I barely recognised her; her hair was salon perfect with silver highlights and not a hint of the yellow peroxide or black roots that she used to favour. She was wearing a very smart black, fitted dress and a pair of matching black velvet court shoes – she told me later that she took both the dress and shoes back to Debenhams the next day for a refund, told them that they didn't fit and amazingly got her money back – and she looked totally transformed and classy and I have to admit that I was very impressed. She looked very upmarket and poised and honestly, I was just waiting for her to open her mouth and spoil it all.

She'd hardly spoken when she arrived, just smiled and said hello and shook Aiden's hand so I had no idea what was coming. She produced a sheet of paper from her handbag and proceeded to give us a sales pitch which she'd written herself (although it sounded vaguely familiar so I have a sneaking suspicion that she copied it from the

Weight Watchers website) in her weird accent that I'd never heard her do before and she totally blew Aiden's, and my, socks off. She was amazing and I couldn't help admiring her determination and ingenuity. Et Voilá! as they say, and the job was hers.

She ditched Charlie along with the dropped aitches, said he was a sponger and she'd seen the light and wasn't having it anymore. Although he didn't go quietly; he kept ringing her constantly and turning up everywhere she went because he couldn't believe that she meant it because she'd dumped him so many times before. He didn't want his meal ticket disappearing because he could never hold down a job and he needed Doris to fund him.

Doris found it all a bit embarrassing, not least because Charlie had started looking a bit rough by then. He'd got into one fight too many and had one of his front teeth knocked out so he definitely didn't fit with the new look Doris. Doe. We were in the throes of the promotion plan for *The Travis Way* and Doris had so far managed to get rid of him when he approached her in the street but he started following her to meetings and waiting around outside Aidan's office until she came out. She was terrified that Charlie would turn up at the promotion venues and show her up. Luckily, Gerald, in his stern lawyer guise, stepped in and threatened Charlie with a restraining order if he didn't leave her alone and that seemed to do the trick – most likely because Charlie already had quite a few outstanding court appearances and was trying to live under the radar.

'When the film's done I'll go back on and announce you – we don't want to overdo it and piss 'em off by playing it again,' Doris whispers in my ear as she squeezes her feet back into her heels. 'You were fab by the way, on the Beeb this morning. Proper natural, like. I'd buy your book if I was fat.'

I whisper my thanks and smile. I take a couple of shaky deep breaths and breathe out slowly and pull my shoulders back in an attempt to quell my nerves. I'll be fine once I'm on the stage because I know the spiel off by heart, it's just the waiting that gets to me. I'll watch the BBC interview later but Gerald has already seen it and phoned me on the way here to assure me that I pitched it just right and that people will be positively scrambling to get their copy of *The Travis Way*. He's so encouraging and even though Aiden does all of the promotional stuff Gerald still takes a keen interest in everything I do.

It's strange when you think about it because the BBC always make a big fuss about not *doing* advertising but the very fact that I appeared on there will have a huge impact on sales. Apparently an appearance on the morning television sofa is worth more than a paid advert anywhere but it's by invitation only; you can't buy it. I was only lucky enough to be invited along because it's fat week, or *Healthy Living Week*, as they call it. And I wouldn't even have been asked if anyone but Aiden had put my name forward. He knows someone on the production team because they were at university together, so it's not what you know it's who you know, obviously.

Apparently I was just what they were looking for because I've changed my life by losing weight and somehow become a bit of a minor celebrity by writing a book about it. The BBC are very politically correct and all about being inclusive so they needed a few normal, non-famous people like me to balance out all of the celebrities that they usually have on the show every morning to peddle their latest film or book.

Today they kicked off fat week with me and a bloke called Warren, who came from Doncaster – the presenters kept referring to this fact as if coming from the north and being on television was something amazing. Warren had lost an incredible thirty-three stone by cycling fifty miles a day. Thirty-three stone, can you imagine? He put me at the bottom of the ladder in the fat stakes because I never weighed as much as he's lost to start with; so it's a sort of fat *top trumps* and he's definitely out trumped me. But this didn't seem to matter, the BBC like to be inclusive and I suppose they had to have a woman on the show to balance out the man so that they couldn't be accused of being discriminating or biased.

I wanted to ask Warren what sort of bike he

had that could cope with someone who weighed nearly fifty stone but I stopped myself; it would have sounded a bit rude but more to the point I didn't want to share my moment in the spotlight with him because I didn't think about asking him until we were live on air. I couldn't help thinking that surely the bike must have been made from reinforced steel or something because a normal road bike couldn't possibly hold that amount of weight, could it? I know nothing about bikes but it seems most unlikely to me. But what I found strange was that the presenters never asked him either and I would have thought that was an obvious question, wouldn't you? I do wonder if he might have been lying about how he lost weight and that really he'd had his stomach stapled or a gastric band fitted because I couldn't help noticing that there wasn't the slightest bit of muscle on his legs; they were a very strange cigar shape with no defined muscle or even a hint of an ankle bone at all and if you were cycling fifty miles a day they'd be super toned, right? From where I was sitting he didn't appear to have any ankles or calves at all.

More to the point, when we were in the green room – the room where they plonk everyone before they're 'live on air' – I watched him as he mashed up an iced doughnut with a spoon and then practically drank it; I can't think of any reason why you would do that unless you had a gastric band or no teeth – and he definitely had teeth. He wielded the fork very deftly too so I think he'd had plenty of practice.

The huge quantity of doughnuts and biscuits provided also made me wonder how serious the BBC really are about *Healthy Eating Week*; not very, I suspect, because they certainly don't practice what they preach.

But who am I to judge? I've not exactly been truthful in *The Travis Way* and no doubt if Warren from Doncaster really *is* lying about how he lost the weight then the press will *out* him sooner or later; it's just a matter of time.

And maybe they'll *out* me, too.

According to Aiden the BBC have lots of other ex-fatties lined up for the rest of the *Healthy Eating Week* and having got Warren and I out of the way the rest of the ex-fatties are celebrities and they all have diet books or exercise DVDs to flog as well. Some of them are on their third or fourth go of losing weight and then putting it back on and then losing it again – although this time they're swearing that this new diet is *the* diet that works and the ones that they did before were rubbish and didn't really work like the new one does.

I did manage to get the fact that I've written a book into almost every sentence that I uttered and the presenters didn't seem to mind at all, they even asked lots of questions about it so I don't know why they don't just put adverts on the BBC and save everyone having to pay the licence fee. I don't mind a few adverts; you can always record it and edit them out or make a cup of tea or something and some of the adverts are more entertaining than the programmes.

The funny thing was that the interview had only just aired and Gerald said that ITV were on the phone to Aiden almost immediately to ask me in for an interview on Thursday – I didn't even need Aiden's contacts to get me a slot on the channel with adverts. ITV are having a healthy eating week too, only they're calling it *Countdown to Summer*, or something like that, because pretty much everyone wants to lose weight and they want to do it easily, without any effort at all because isn't that exactly how I did it and it's all there for the taking in *The Travis Way.*

I thought that I was the only one to be obsessed with being fat and dieting but it seems pretty much the whole world is on a diet or thinking about going on a diet or has just been on a diet. The make-up girl at the BBC told me she was on a diet; she was wafer thin with not an ounce of fat anywhere on her but as she brushed highlighter onto my face she happily related how she only had one more stone to lose before she reached her ideal weight. She was very interested to hear about my book and said she fully intended reading it and was definitely going to try my diet after she finished the one she was on now, which was the high fat no carbs one, so that she could maintain her weight when she'd lost that last stone. She liked the idea of *my non-diet diet* and said that if she hadn't already bought all of her steak, cheese and cream for the week she would have tried mine straight away.

I couldn't see that she needed to lose any more weight and I think maybe she had an eating disorder (obviously I didn't say that bit) and when I told her how lovely and slim she looked she looked at me in absolute disbelief. *Look at this roll of fat!* She shrieked as she stood back from the chair and pulled up her jumper and grabbed a scrawny piece of skin between her thumb and index finger, *Disgusting!* Her eyes were filled with loathing for herself and I felt sorry for her then because I realised that in her eyes she'd never be thin enough even though she was practically skeletal. Also, as she shrieked right into my face I got a blast of breath that could stop a bus because that's what the high fat no carbs diet does for you and sadly us dieters think that bad breath is a price worth paying; no pain, no gain.

Or should that be un-gain?

'Al.' I feel Doris nudge me in the ribs with her elbow.

I look at her in confusion, wondering where on earth I am.

'You ready?' She's looking at me with concern, her flawless micro-bladed eyebrows furrowed over her perfectly made up blue eyes.

'I'm fine.' I manage a fake smile and take a deep breath. 'Miles away.'

'Well don't doze off and miss your cue or I'll look a right prick.'

I smile and give her a double thumbs up.

Doris smooths down the non-existent creases in her dress with her perfectly manicured hands, gives me a wink and struts onto the stage in her sparkly stilettos, the pale pink skirt on her dress swinging jauntily. She pauses briefly to take the microphone from the stand like a true pro and moves closer to the front of the stage.

'Inspiring, isn't it?' She announces breathily into the microphone whilst directing a beaming smile at the audience. 'And for those of you eager to follow in Alison's footsteps we have a limited supply of *The Travis Way* on sale in the foyer today at the special price of only fourteen pounds ninety-nine, an absolute bargain as I'm sure you'll agree. Just fourteen pounds ninety-nine to change your life forever!' She pauses to let this sink in before continuing. 'Alison will also be staying for a short while afterwards to autograph copies of her book before she has to dash off for another television interview, so do make sure that you're the first in the queue if you want to be sure of meeting her personally.'

This is a lie, I don't have to dash off anywhere because the ITV interview isn't until Thursday but according to Aiden if you're too available people don't want you; they like to think that you're super busy and important and that they've been extremely fortunate that you had the time to even bother speaking to them as you take their money off them.

If you lie when you're selling something is it lying or does lying only count in real life? Advertising seems to me like one big lie but somehow it's viewed as perfectly acceptable, even mandatory. From the digitally enhanced photographs to make you look worse or better depending on the requirement, to the ridiculous results claimed in my book, no one bats an eyelid or even considers that it's lying; it's *advertising.*

I used to feel bad for lying because although I'd become very good at it and actually thoroughly enjoyed it, I thought it was morally wrong and that I needed to stop because it's not what a good person would do.

But now I'm not so sure.

So, no interviews today, I'm actually going home to my beautifully furnished, expensive, apartment to catch up on some extremely important emails from my growing list of loyal fans. This is also a complete lie but it's what I've told Doris and Gerald and Aiden because I obviously can't tell them the truth.

Which is that I'm going to go home and gorge myself on crisps and chocolate and anything else that I can lay my hands on because I've barely eaten for three days and I'm absolutely starving. This will of course be after I've donned a disguise of dark glasses and headscarf so that I can visit a shop outside of Frogham where hopefully no one will recognise me, so that I can purchase my forbidden food without anyone knowing. My mouth waters at the thought of the treats in store and I hastily swallow it down; I don't want to go on stage drooling like a madman.

'Ladies and gentlemen.' Doris holds her arm out towards me. 'I give you, Alison Travis.'

I take a deep breath and pull my mouth into a huge smile; time to go. I push back my shoulders and glide onto the stage to tumultuous applause.

CHAPTER TWO

I stayed for over two hours after the presentation to sign copies of my book; the queue of people was so long that I felt I couldn't just go. They were buying a book based on a lie and the very least I could do was autograph it for them. Aiden had kindly arranged for two more cardboard cut outs of fat me to be placed on each side of the table where I was sitting so that while people were waiting for my autograph they could fully witness the massive difference between then and now - which would therefore make them more willing to part with fourteen pounds ninety-nine.

I remember very clearly the day that I took that photograph; I went into my bedroom just after I'd given Mother her breakfast and I stood in front of the mirror and snapped a picture on my phone. I certainly had no intention of ever letting anyone else see it, it was most definitely for my eyes only. It was the morning that I weighed myself after my first week of dieting and discovered that I'd lost eight pounds. I remember being absolutely thrilled with myself and so excited about starting my new life and so sure that *this* time the diet was going to work and I was going to transform myself and also somehow find and make friends with Bella.

I have to confess that I now feel mortally embarrassed about my stalking of Bella and my desperation to befriend her and to mould myself into a version of her. Thank God that no one knows about that because I think I'd just die if anyone found out about it. Quite honestly, I'd rather have gone to prison for the attempted murder of Rita than admit to a massive crush on another woman. Because it definitely was a crush, I can see that quite clearly now and honestly, I cringe just thinking about it.

Who would have guessed where I'd be less than eighteen months later? Sometimes I wish that I'd never taken that photograph because it's absolutely *everywhere* and I'll never get away from it because once it's on the internet it's there forever. Even when my book is a dim and distant memory that hideous photograph will still be there to remind anyone who cares to look just how fat I used to be.

But the sensible part of me knows that it's fortunate that I *did* take it otherwise there'd be no *before* picture and they're vital in the world of diet books so that you can prove just how enormous and miserable you were before you shed the blubber.

Although I've no doubt that Aiden would have faked a photo if necessary; I think he can pretty much arrange or obtain anything.

Talking of Bella, I bumped into her a few weeks ago. Okay, I didn't *actually* bump into her I put my trusty sunglasses and headscarf disguise on and trundled around to Brothertons Estate Agents to have a look through the window at her. I don't know why, really, I just started thinking about things and my curiosity got the better of me and I wanted to see if she was as perfect as I remembered her.

She wasn't, as it turned out. She'd put on a fair bit of weight due to the fact that she was heavily pregnant and looked about ready to drop. To say she looked rough might be stretching it a bit but she certainly didn't look too hot and trust me; no one would hold her up as a role model now. Her face was a bit spotty and blotchy and her hair was lank and lifeless and in need of a good shampooing. I should have felt very superior as I watched her lumbering around the office with her massive bump because I look *so* much better than her now but I didn't, I just felt jealous; not because she was pregnant but because she looked so *happy* and obviously didn't care one jot about how she looked.

I'm guessing that her and Justin Smarty Pants got over the *porn on the works laptop* thing and are happily waiting for their perfect child to arrive so he or she can complete their perfect life. No doubt the baby will be born beautiful and clever and the cycle of charmed lives will continue.

I could have saved myself the journey and found out what she was up to by looking at her emails if I'd not panicked and destroyed everything to do with her – and Justin. Once Gerald had secured my release from the police station I was so terrified that I might be arrested again that I deleted everything from my laptop. I then thought maybe that wasn't enough so I pulled the hard drive out of it and bashed it with the same hammer that I used to break open Mother's drawer. It wouldn't break even though I battered it repeatedly and I still had my doubts about whether I'd destroy all the evidence on there so I immersed it in a bucket of bleach for a week and then put it inside a chicken carcass and threw it in the bin. Probably totally over the top but you can never be too careful, can you? I felt relieved to be rid of it and it marked the start of my new post Mother and post Bella life; I also treated myself to a brand new top of the range laptop to replace it because even if I hadn't panicked about the evidence I would have thrown it out because I refuse to have anything *budget* in my life now. My whole life has been spent making do and having the cheapest of everything and I'm never doing that again.

I still have moments of panic about it all even though if anything was going to happen it would have happened by now. It's probably just as well that I can't read Bella's emails because I don't want to go getting obsessed again – I don't think I would but you never know.

Seeing Bella looking happy and contented and not caring what she looked like made me think - isn't that how we should all be, why should appearances matter so much? I thought how I looked and what I weighed was the most important thing in the world and that once I'd lost weight my life would be perfect but it's not.

So, anyway, back to my book signing - I think nearly every person in that theatre bought my book; some even bought two copies, one for themselves and one for a friend or for their sister or mother who was also looking for the magic answer to their weight problem. And they were all women; As far as I could see there wasn't one man amongst the whole audience. What does that say? Okay, Warren at the BBC was an ex-fattie but he's the exception because mostly it's women that are obsessed with their weight and how they look, not men. I bet if you did some sort of survey to find out the percentage of men who are discontent about their weight it would be miniscule compared to the number of women who hate themselves.

As I scribbled my signature in the books my smile became more and more fixed and I felt worse and worse and I just wanted to run away. My mouth was so dry that my teeth kept sticking to my lips and I feel sure I must have looked slightly unhinged but no one seemed to notice; all those women could see was someone who'd once been fat and was now slim; fat girl slim. I was like them, you see, so even though they still had loads of weight to lose they didn't feel judged by me because I used to be just like them and I was their inspiration.

And people were so *nice* to me; asking me how I was and if I still followed the plan to make sure I stayed the same size and I lied through my teeth and said *of course* and I saw the hopeful way that they looked at me and I thought, *if only you knew*. They didn't feel embarrassed about their size talking to me because I was their sister in fatness and I understood how they felt. I gave them hope that they too could transform their lives the easy way with *The Travis Plan*.

Honestly, it was enough to drive me straight to the biscuit tin although that's not an excuse because I'd already decided way before then that I was going to stuff my face when I got home. I've barely eaten a thing for three days in readiness for my BBC interview and my ITV interview isn't until Thursday so I have Tuesday and Wednesday to starve off tonight's binge to feel thin again.

Not that those people shelling out fourteen pounds ninety-nine know this; they really believe that my book will change their lives and whilst I'm not averse to lying, as you know, I felt like a heel because they were all looking for the magic answer to their weight problem and my book was going to provide the solution, because wasn't I the living proof?

Because I have kept it off, there's absolutely no doubt about that; I'm ultra slim and a walking, talking success story for losing weight and staying slim.

But the book?

The book is a big fat lie.

Or a big skinny lie, depending on your point of view.

The book doesn't tell how I really lost weight at all.

It's all Gerald's fault, the book. Although at first I thought it was a fantastic idea if I'm being honest; which I'm not, most of the time.

After Mother died and the police had released me and I realised that I'd got away with nearly murdering Rita, unintentionally of course, I threw myself into organising a brand new life for myself. And at first it *was* fantastic but, after the excitement of selling the house and buying and furnishing my nice swish apartment was over I was at a bit of a loose end.

It was such fun buying everything I wanted for my apartment; no recycled seventies tat for me - I bought the very best of everything and all brand, spanking new. I'd got a fantastic price for the house – far more than I ever dreamed of – because two building companies were both vying for it because it was an ideal plot for turning into apartments because of the huge garden. It eventually sold for fifty thousand pounds more than the price it had gone on the market for which was incredible. I went back to have look a couple of months ago to see what they'd done and although only the foundations were down I could see that they'd extended all of the way into the hated, overgrown back garden. There was a big board up advertising four luxury apartments with their own parking; from the advertised prices they're still going to make a huge profit even though they overpaid me massively. It bore no resemblance at all to the miserable, cheerless house that I'd been brought up in and as I looked at the foundations I struggled to picture the house in my mind and that dreaded cellar seemed a distant, horrible memory.

And to have so much money and never to want for anything again – unless I'm really stupid and start gambling or throw money away I'm set up for life. I can't describe the feeling of walking into a shop and just buying whatever I want after years of making do - and I thought I'd never, ever tire of it but of course I have. There comes a point when you have absolutely everything you need and looking around shops becomes a bit of a bore because there is nothing else that you actually *want*. I have wardrobes packed chockfull of designer clothes and I can never hope to wear even half of them before they go out of fashion; I probably have more clothes than Bella did.

Gerald kept offering to find a suitable job for me so I'd have something to do. He said he'd have a word with his various friends who all have their own businesses and were always looking for *good people* to take onboard because according to him I'd be just what they were looking for. He doesn't see me like I really am because I don't have any skills at all apart from cleaning but I didn't want to disillusion him so I said I'd think about it. He even suggested that when I did eventually find something that I wanted to do I should employ a cleaner so that I wouldn't have the burden of housework. I said I couldn't possibly do that because I just loved cleaning and looking after my lovely new apartment myself was an absolute pleasure.

Complete tosh of course but no way was I letting a cleaner in to snoop around my personal belongings; I know they're not all like me but really, why take the chance?

I knew that I needed to get a job; not for the salary but because retiring at twenty-nine is not a good thing to do.

Or so Gerald kept telling me.

I needed a career, he said, a job that would give me somewhere to use my skills and give me something to get my teeth into, but the thing was, I really couldn't be bothered. I also didn't have any skills, apart from being a good liar (so maybe I could have gone into advertising) and being a cleaner, so I'd have to do some sort of training or go to university which I always thought I would love to do, given half a chance, but after browsing through a few prospectuses I quickly realised that I wasn't interested.

All far too much like hard work.

Also, I have unresolved issues that I need to work through.

Namely Mother and my late father.

Once Mother was dead that really should have been the end of it, shouldn't it? I spent most of my life secretly hoping that she'd either have a complete personality change and decide to love me or failing that, die. Well, once she was dead I was as free as a bird but I came to realise after a while that I didn't quite know what to do with this new found freedom that I'd longed for; in a strange way I missed looking after her because I'd done it for so long and it was all I'd ever known in my adult life.

Not that I wanted her back, God forbid, absolutely not.

There was also the elephant in the room that I was ignoring: my late father's box of tat from the nursing home that I hadn't yet had the guts to open. It's still there, a battered tea chest, sitting in the corner of my smallest bedroom with a throw arranged neatly over it to hide it. I haven't had the nerve to open it and I had absolutely no intention of even collecting it from the home but Gerald took it upon himself to pick it up and bring it round. He thought he was helping, bless him.

So. I should go through it and sort it all out and then bin it; no doubt it's full of old spectacles, broken hearing aids and photographs of people that I don't even know.

But I can't bring myself to.

And I can't seem to make myself throw it out without sorting through it either, so it would have been better all round if Gerald had left it at the home and then I wouldn't need to make a decision about it.

So there it is; I'm not only a liar but a coward too and I can't blame Mother for that because she was many things but you could never call her a coward.

So I know I have issues and just as I was thinking about maybe getting some counselling to gird me into *doing something with my life*, two things happened. Well, three things really.

Firstly, I discovered that getting slim was all very well but staying slim was a different matter altogether. Now down to an extremely slim size eight, I didn't want or need to lose any more weight so I thought I'd go back to eating normally and just stay the same. Not eating normally as in binging on chocolate and crisps and anything else I could get my hands on but eating like I used to before I got massively fat – you know, normal sized meals with the odd treat thrown in now and then. Which meant eating when I was hungry and not obsessing over what I was shoving down my throat or ramming it in even if I didn't want it because I *had* to eat everything in sight because I'd spent the previous three days starving myself.

So I dispensed with the starving and binging and it was such a relief to eat normally after starving myself for so long; I ate small portions and didn't binge at all and I felt rather pleased with myself because I was being *normal,* how I used to be before I was fat. I was starting to enjoy eating again and the compulsion to binge was gradually receding and I thought *I can do this*. I even started to think that maybe I *could* open that Pandora's box of my father's belongings because if I could eat normally who knew what else I could achieve?

But I soon discovered that normal didn't work for me, maybe it does for other people but not me. After a few weeks I noticed that my lovely new clothes were getting a bit tight and getting into my skinny jeans became a struggle. I had to lie on the bed to zip them up and I could hardly breathe when I stood up and I thought I was going to pass out. Maybe I wasn't meant to be this thin, the sensible part of me said, maybe *my* normal is a bit bigger than a size eight but not jumbo sized like I used to be. Because when I thought about it I remembered that when I was eighteen I was a size twelve - a perfectly normal, acceptable size and I was quite happy as I was then. Not super slim, or model girl slim but *normal size:* I realised that most likely the only time that I'd ever been a size eight before was when I was about ten years old.

But the un-sensible part didn't like that. No, it said, you can be super slim if you put more effort in, you need to try harder - you're just being *lazy and greedy*. Okay, I conceded, maybe I am so I know what I'll do – I'll go out running because it worked before and I *had* let the running slip, mostly because I now didn't need to leave the house to run for hours and hours to escape from Mother.

And I did go back to running for a week or two but my heart wasn't really in it; I just couldn't get the motivation back that I'd once had and I kept making excuses to myself to not go and before I knew it the old feelings of being out of control and being disgusted with myself started to rear their ugly fat heads again.

So. Basically I had a choice, eat normally and be a size twelve-ish or starve myself for the rest of my life to stay a super slim size eight. And I was giving this problem serious thought when the second thing happened.

Gerald asked me to marry him.

I was completely gobsmacked. Gerald and I had become very close; he is a true friend to me and once you get past the constant talking and showing off he really is a complete sweetheart, but marriage? He'd never even told me he loved me and even though he asked me to marry him he never said he loved me then, either, he asked in a very business-like, lawyerly way. Maybe I expect too much and people don't bother telling each other that they love each other nowadays because I really wouldn't know, would I?

The thing was we hadn't even had sex – I kept putting him off, told him that I wasn't ready and I needed to sort myself out and the usual clichéd old guff but if anything it had made him even more attracted to me. Did he ask me to marry him so I'd have sex with him – was that the plan?

And then once I'd slept with him he'd call the engagement off? I know that I'm far too suspicious and the rational part of me knew I was being ridiculous and that Gerald is far too honourable to do that. But that's the thing, you see, I have so little life experience that I suspect people's motives constantly. And the thing is I don't know why I didn't sleep with him – he is very attractive when he stops talking and quite masterful when he's in full lawyer mode so I don't understand it myself really because he's gorgeous.

Yes I do, I'm lying again. I didn't have sex with him because I was frightened of what would happen – I really was afraid that we'd have a brief affair, he'd get bored with me after the novelty had worn off and then we wouldn't be friends anymore and I didn't want that to happen; I wanted him in my life because apart from Doris he's the only friend I've got.

Although I haven't exactly been celibate since Mother died, although obviously Gerald doesn't know about that and will hopefully never find out. Fingers crossed.

Anyway, I told him I'd have to think about it and I *did* give it a lot of thought and part of me wanted to say yes, because then I wouldn't have to think about what to do with my life because it would all be taken out of my hands; Gerald would be a sort of a replacement for Mother only much nicer, of course. And I'd just not have sex with him until we were actually married so he couldn't jilt me.

So I dithered around and after a few weeks I'd decided two things; firstly, that I was going to eat normally and if I put on a bit of weight, so be it; and secondly I was going to marry Gerald and have a normal life to go with my normal eating. The bonus of getting married was that I wouldn't have to think about a career or getting a job because obviously Gerald would want a family and I could have a baby or two and maybe even look after them when the nanny was off duty. But obviously we'd have lots of holidays and fun before that and we'd also have to move to a nice big house which would need furnishing and making into a nice home which would give me something to occupy my days.

I felt very pleased with myself for being so grown up and making two such important decisions and was just about to tell Gerald *yes* when the third thing happened which basically cancelled out the two decisions that I'd made.

Somehow, Gerald found out that I used to be fat. I'd never told him for obvious reasons, because I wasn't exactly proud of how I used to be but also because I had a feeling it would put him right off me. I don't know who told him because apart from Doris, who he had only met briefly then, I didn't have any friends who could have told him but somehow he'd discovered my fat past.

I was horrified that he knew because I felt this altered his perception of me; he also seemed far too interested in me having been fat for my liking and we nearly had our very first row because he couldn't understand why I hadn't told him. I said it was because I was ashamed but for some reason he seemed to find it fascinating that I had once been huge. He kept on and on about it so much that in a fit of temper I thumbed through my phone and showed him the now famous picture of *fat me* that's plastered all over the internet.

As he studied the picture I could tell by the look on his face that when he'd thought I was fat he had absolutely no idea how huge I'd really been. His idea of fat was probably a perfectly normal size fourteen and as I watched him study the picture I could see the look of pity and disgust on his face even though he tried his best to hide it.

It was the very same look that I'd seen on so many faces before and I quickly realised that I'd been a complete fool to show him the photograph because there were no others and he'd never have known how massive I'd really been and could only have guessed.

I never did tell him *yes* because I knew that there'd be no chance of him marrying me now and he never mentioned his proposal again - so don't tell me that looks don't matter and it's what's on the inside that counts because it's not true.

The only good thing that came out of Gerald seeing that photograph was *The Travis Way*.

At least I thought it was a good thing at the time.

* * *

Like most diet books *The Travis Way* is basically a rehash of all of the other diet books around. Eat less – a lot less – it informs you, and you will, eventually - if you can stick to it long enough - lose a ton of weight if you don't die of boredom first. It doesn't tell you that the thought of food will occupy your every living moment and that you'll spend all of your days thinking about food and planning what you can have for your next meal and calculating how much weight you're going to lose or that dieting will be pretty much all you ever want to talk about. It doesn't tell you that your whole life will be dictated to by the scales and that a loss or gain of a pound will govern your entire mood for the day; it doesn't tell you that you'll be feeling great and convinced that you've lost a few pounds but that the minute you step on the scales to find that you haven't lost an ounce your day will be totally destroyed. No, it doesn't tell you any of that because obviously the truth doesn't sell books.

And every diet needs an angle, something new, or packaged as new. You must have seen them all; no carbs, the soup only diet, the no eating food but lots of disgusting shakes diet, eat what you like for three days and less for four diet, the eat as much lettuce and vegetables as you can stomach diet, you get the general idea. And they all definitely work if you can stick to them for long enough.

So when Gerald had this brilliant idea about me writing a diet book I had to come up with a gimmick because obviously the way that I really got slim wouldn't sell; running for miles and miles every day and starving myself for days at a time. Living on black coffee and not much else was not what people wanted to hear or would pay good money for. No, it had to be a diet that required very little exercise with clearly defined limits on food intake and would definitely work if you stuck to it forever.

So I came up with *The Travis Way*.

Quite brilliant, though I say it myself, and I sold it to Gerald and he totally believed it so everyone else would too because the proof that the diet works is right in front of you.

Me.

It was quite easy to write the basics of the book and only took an evening on the internet whilst I was watching television and once I'd come up with the *not eating until lunchtime* gimmick the rest of it was easy. Not eating until lunchtime means there's less time to consume calories and with only two meals a day there's less time to stuff your face.

I came up with lots of meal ideas and recipes which I filched off various other diet plans and jumbled up the ingredients a bit so it wouldn't be obvious where I'd got them from and there it was: *The Travis Way*. I also added in twenty minutes a day of gentle exercise – a brisk walk or a gentle bike ride because obviously people wouldn't want to be pounding the streets for hours on end like I did. I never mentioned calories of course, because people don't want to hear about that but all of the meals were mostly vegetables with a tiny bit of meat thrown in so you'd be guaranteed to lose weight.

If you could stick to it.

I'd always imagined that to get a book published would take forever but in a matter of weeks *The Travis Way* was on the shelves and selling like hot cakes; the power of not what you know but who you know. Gerald, obviously, not me, because I don't know anyone.

And I never imagined for one minute that it would be so successful or that I would become a prisoner of *The Travis Way* as much as I was a prisoner of Mother.

Because I can never put weight on now, can I?

I have to stay a size eight forever.

CHAPTER THREE

The Virginian Bar and Grill is a sea of polished chrome, blonde wood and sparkling cutlery. The artful lighting dances on the polished metal and the low music is jazzy horns and moody wailing; the atmosphere says that you're lucky to be here and you must behave in the appropriate manner. It's full of customers with far too much money wearing expensive designer clothing who want to be seen in all of the best restaurants and The Virginian is definitely one of the best. Aiden booked us a table for lunch and was, according to him, very lucky to get one as not just anyone can ring up and get a table, just like that.

He name dropped me – isn't that hilarious? The fact that I would be fresh from my interview at the ITV television studios meant a table for three was miraculously secured for the fourth row from the front – which is the second row from the back so not quite at the bottom of the celebrity ladder but pretty low down. I'm just about hanging onto the *famous* scale by my fingertips but I'm obviously not well known enough to get a table near the door or window where the real celebrities are seated. If today had been a Saturday or a Sunday instead of a Thursday we most likely wouldn't have a table at all.

We've already ordered our food – a salad for me, of course, a barely cooked steak for Gerald and poached salmon for Aiden. I'm nursing a glass of fizzy mineral water whilst Gerald slurps on a million calorie cocktail that looks so much more enticing than my boring water. Aiden could have whatever drink he wants but in typical boring Aiden fashion he's chosen to drink tap water.

That's the curse of having written a diet book; absolutely everything that you put into your mouth is scrutinised and because the whole world has a mobile phone you never know when someone's going to whip it out to snap a picture of you eating a cream cake or a bar of chocolate and plaster it all over social media. Stuffing of high calorie foods, in fact any food that isn't a salad, is for behind closed doors only. I've forgone wine too in my quest to look health conscious; no matter, I have wine at home which I will open to go with the fish and chips than I plan to purchase on my way home tonight.

Gerald is looking rather gorgeous and darkly handsome today in a dark blue suit with a button down pale blue shirt with matching tie and for once he isn't talking but silently studying the wine list. Doris's description of him as *well fit* is exactly right and when he's not *going on* I definitely fancy the pants off him. I really shouldn't have dithered when he asked me to marry him, I should have said *yes* straight away before he'd had a chance to change his mind. Although he'd probably have called off the engagement after he'd seen the picture of *fat me.* Not that he's told me he's changed his mind – he's far too well-mannered to do that but the fact that he hasn't produced an engagement ring or mentioned his proposal again says all I need to know. A sigh escapes me and Gerald looks up from the list of over-priced reds and looks at me with concern.

'Something wrong, darling?' He asks in a worried tone. He still always calls me *darling,* so maybe there's a little bit of hope that he doesn't find me completely disgusting. Or it could just be that he's being very polite; he has impeccable manners.

'No, I'm fine,' I say with a smile as I pick up my hated mineral water and take a ladylike sip.

Gerald folds the menu closed and places it flat on the table and rests his perfectly manicured hands carefully on top of it.

'Now, darling, you're not upset about that awful man from Doncaster are you?' He pulls a disgusted face and I stifle a giggle under a pretend cough.

'No, not at all, he couldn't help it. I felt a bit sorry for him to be honest. It must have been awful.'

Gerald smiles. 'You're far too nice darling, especially as he brought it on himself.'

I suppose he did. Gerald had the day off so he came with me to the studios and when we were in the ITV green room before my interview, Warren, the cycling dieter from Doncaster, could barely contain his excitement when they brought in the refreshments. Ignoring the pots of tea and coffee on offer he'd made a beeline for the cakes. Not doughnuts this time; ITV had pushed the boat out and there were fresh cream chocolate éclairs, creams horns, rum babas, every cream cake that I'd ever seen and a few that were new to me. I'd relayed the story about the iced doughnut to Gerald so he was taking a keen interest in Warren and the cake situation. Warren wasn't making much of an effort to hide what he was doing; he would walk casually past the cake table several times and each time he'd pick up a couple of cakes because the plates were nearly empty after a few walk bys. I don't know whether he stuffed them in his pockets or he had a bag he hid them in but wherever they were the table was nearly bare by the time he finally sat down. His seat was in the furthest corner of the room and was partially obscured by a pillar so we couldn't actually see what he was doing but no doubt he mashed them all up with a fork and drank them down.

Not that anyone else was going to eat them, everyone was far too nervous about their impending television appearance and one lady

(Weight Watchers slimmer of the year) choked on her cup of tea and sprayed it everywhere. It would have been much better if they'd bought the cakes out *after* we'd been on air and then everyone could have tucked in and enjoyed them.

Personally, I think the canteen did it on purpose so they could have all of the leftovers for themselves because by the time we'd finished our interviews the few remaining cakes that Warren hadn't eaten had all been whisked away along with the tea and coffee pots. The studio manager said we were all welcome to use the green room until we were ready to leave but there wasn't a lot of point as there wasn't even a glass of water to be had.

'What did the man from Doncaster do?' Aiden asks in a bored tone from across the table. He tucks his phone into the top pocket of his jacket which signals his willingness to join in the conversation; he didn't even look up from the screen to give the waiter his food order but barked it out in his monotone manner while his eyes were still fixed to the screen.

Very rude, I think, but then Aiden *is* rude; sometimes if I ask him a question he doesn't even answer but half an hour later he'll reply to me as if I've asked him only seconds before.

When I arrived Gerald and Aiden were already here and whereas Gerald got up from his seat to kiss and greet me, Aiden simply glanced up for a millisecond and then resumed his looking at his phone.

'Um, he had a bit of an accident.' Gerald coughs in embarrassment.

'Accident?' Aiden raises his eyebrows at Gerald.

'Yes, it was a bit unfortunate,' I say.

Aiden totally ignores me and I see his fingers twitching towards his jacket pocket.

'He shit himself,' I add in a flat voice.

Aiden's hand freezes on its journey to his pocket and I see his Adam's apple bob on his long skinny white neck as he struggles to swallow. Maybe it was spiteful of me to state it so bluntly because Aiden is squeamish to the extreme; I've witnessed him nearly vomit when he accidently stepped on a dog turd on the pavement. I've most likely ruined his salmon for him now because it's unlikely he'll be able to eat after the vision I've conjured up for him.

'All over the *Breakfast Time* sofa. Went everywhere.' I continue, just to make sure he gets the complete picture and there's no ambiguity.

Aiden doesn't speak but quickly pushes his chair back and the chair legs screech across the wooden floor and the sound reverberates around the room. He stands up and hurriedly excuses himself to Gerald - but not me, and heads off towards the gents at a semi-trot. Honestly, I know I'm being nasty but I can't help myself sometimes, he's such an arse. God knows how he's so good at advertising and marketing because he's probably the most unsociable person in the world and has no social skills whatsoever. He's the absolute dullest person that I've ever met - from his never changing attire of black suit and white shirt, which always looks brand new, so he must have hundreds of them – to his blank expression which veers between not interested and faintly disgusted and I've never witnessed him smile. He only speaks when *he* wants to and has absolutely no sense of humour either. I don't think I've ever had a conversation with him that's not about promoting my book and then it's mostly him doing the talking because whenever I start to speak he cuts across me as if I'm an idiot.

The only time I've seen him in the slightest bit animated is when he's around Doris; his vampire pale skin acquires the merest hint of colour and he can't take his eyes off her. Doris hadn't even noticed and when I told her she thought it was hilarious, *Aiden?* She'd screamed between hoots of laughter, *he's proper weird,* well, he might be weird I'd said, but he's definitely got the hots for you. This produced yet more shrieks of laughter, *Na,* she said when she finally stopped laughing, *I shouldn't fink he's got a shag in 'im*

Another reason I dislike him is that he's rasher thin and actually leaves food on his plate when he's eaten enough, even if it's only a mouthful because apparently *when he's had sufficient, why continue?* He informed me of this in his robotic way when I asked him if there was something wrong with the teaspoonful of Moussaka he'd left on his plate when we were having lunch one day. Not normal is it? I have to clear the plate, hungry or not, and certainly wouldn't leave a *mouthful*. I know this is a completely un-rational reason to dislike him, but there it is.

'Oh dear.' Gerald smirks. 'Poor Aiden and his glass stomach. Lucky he wasn't being interviewed on the sofa with you or they'd have had vomit to contend with as well.'

We laugh guiltily and I think that maybe Gerald doesn't like Aiden very much either, even though he's supposedly one of his friends.

The thing is, I didn't even realise at first what had happened with Warren – I was giving my well-practised spiel about *The Travis Way* to the presenters and doing it with a lot more confidence than I had at the BBC on Monday, when the most awful stench hit my nostrils. I lost track of what I was saying just for a moment but soon recovered and finished my piece, but out of the corner of my eye I was aware of some sort of kerfuffle at the other end of the sofa where Warren was sitting. I didn't dare turn my head in case the camera was still on me so I fixed my eyes on the presenter as she hurriedly announced a commercial break. As soon as the floor manager shouted *break* the whole studio erupted into action.

I looked over at Warren then because it seemed as if the entire breakfast team were converging on his end of the sofa. An overall-ed lady with a mop and a bucket appeared from a cupboard somewhere and started to make her way over but was frantically waved back by the floor manager. One of the runners hurried over to me and asked me to move off the sofa and stand out of the way so I jumped up and stood and watched from a safe distance as I didn't want any of it splattering on my clothes.

Warren must have been whisked away because he was nowhere to be seen but the evidence of all of the cakes was spread over a good three foot of the sofa and dripping onto the floor - the smell was absolutely horrific. That's when I realised that the sofa was in four sections because the section Warren had been sitting on was pulled out and carried away at arm's length by four men – this was after it had been covered with a huge sheet of polythene. The same four men appeared minutes later with a new, clean, sofa section and waited while the cleaner got to work with her mop and bucket on the floor. By the time the commercial break was over the new sofa was in situ and a standby guest had been wheeled out for interview and it was as if Warren had never been there at all. Apart from the smell; even with all of the air freshener the runners were squirting everywhere it still smelled like a public toilet.

Poor Warren, I did feel for him, the only good thing was that he wasn't on air at the time – the camera was on me so thankfully only the studio staff witnessed his humiliation.

Until someone sells their story to the tabloids

of course; maybe he'll have a few days grace before that happens.

I never saw Warren after that, I guess he would have been given a change of clothing and sent on his way. I don't imagine he'll be doing any more interviews and it'll just be a matter of time now before he's outed as a secret gastric bander and his disgrace will be complete; maybe the tabloids will do a feature, *the drawbacks of a gastric band* or something like that.

I do wonder how successful a gastric band as a form of weight loss is if you're prepared to mash up stuff just so you can get it down your throat. Can you say a diet or surgery works if it doesn't stop the craving for food? Because if you're still craving the very food you're cutting out then it's only a matter of time before you're going to fall off the wagon and stuff your face until you can barely breathe.

I watch as Aiden silently weaves his way back to the table from his trip to the gents; when he reaches his chair he silently pulls it out from the table and lowers himself gingerly onto it as if he were a frail ninety year old recovering from major surgery.

'You okay, Aiden?' Gerald looks at Aiden with sympathy but I can see the merest hint of a smirk on his face.

Aiden ignores him and takes his glasses off, pulls a small cloth from his jacket pocket and proceeds to thoroughly polish the lenses.

See? Just rude.

Gerald says nothing and picks the wine list up and moves it to the opposite side of the table from Aiden.

'Perhaps we'll give the wine a miss today.'

Aiden ignores him and continues to polish his already sparkling glasses and we sit in silence until we're interrupted by the arrival of the waiter holding two plates aloft.

'Madam.' The waiter places my salad in front of me and with one hand expertly turns the plate around to better showcase the totally boring collection of lettuce leaves.

'Sir?' The waiter raises an eyebrow at Gerald, who nods and the waiter places his rare, bloody steak on the table in front of him and the swivelling is repeated. Another waiter has appeared next to Aiden and is just about to place his salmon in front of him when the loud screech of chair legs echoes around the room again. I watch as Aiden near runs towards the gents with his hand clamped over his mouth.

'I think you'd better take that away,' Gerald says to the waiter, who silently picks up the plate and glides away.

* * *

Aiden did eventually come back to the table although Gerald and I had nearly finished our meals by then. He looked even paler than before and kept wiping his lips with a tissue. He averted his eyes as Gerald finished the last of his steak and with a shaking hand poured himself another glass of water from the jug and took miniscule sips interspersed with more dabbing of the lips.

God he's annoying.

Once the plates and all traces of food were removed he seemed to recover and his grey face returned to its normal death-like pallor and he became more talkative.

One of the tabloids had approached him, he said – or did he approach them? I forget because his robotic drone bores me to death and I have to keep reminding myself to listen to him instead of falling asleep. He's so boring that by comparison he's making me think that Gerald doesn't *go on* as much as I think he does and that maybe I just expect too much. Anyway, Aiden is negotiating with a daily national newspaper to serialise *The Travis Way* and the plan is that every day they'll print a selection of the recipes along with repeating the not eating before lunchtime gimmick. My immediate response to Aiden is that it'll stop people from buying my book, because why pay fourteen pounds ninety-nine when you can get the book for the price of a daily newspaper - or free if you read it online?

Aiden gives me that look, the *don't be stupid* look that he gives me whenever I ask him a question. He doesn't exactly roll his eyes and sigh because he never shows emotion but he stares into space for a moment and presses his lips even more tightly together before he finally speaks.

'No. It'll increase sales,' he states robotically.

'How?' I snap.

He repeats the stare and lip pressing. 'When the public see the first instalment of the book they won't want to wait until the next day for another instalment and they won't want to keep bits of old newspaper lying around. Research has shown that when people decide to start a diet they want to start immediately and they don't mind paying for it. Trust me, they'll buy the book because it's cheap. It's a win-win, because the newspaper will be *paying* us to serialise *The Travis Way* but they'll also be giving us free publicity at the same time.'

I don't think the book's cheap but maybe that's because I know that it's a cut and paste job off the internet; it's not exactly good value for money but in my desperate try anything, pre-weight loss days I'd probably have bought it too.

'Okay,' I say, 'Let's go for it.' I might hate him but he does know his stuff.

Aiden nods almost imperceptibly.

'Now. Woman of the Year.'

'Why thank you, Aiden, very nice of you to say so.'

He ignores my attempt at a joke and continues to drone on.

'The Woman of the Year Awards are next week and with great difficulty I've managed to procure two tickets; it's most definitely going to be *the* place to be seen. The paparazzi will be in full attendance at the entrance and anyone who's anyone will be there. If you get yourself noticed there then you'll most likely get asked by one of the women's magazines for a feature. Your *poor fat girl loses weight and is now rich* story will fit just right with them. You need to make sure that you get yourself a knock out dress by an up and coming designer so that you look the part – I can supply you with a list of names of suitable dressers. No outrageous outfits or showing too much flesh, you need to look like a successful dieter, not a tart. They'll probably lend it you for free provided you name drop them if you're interviewed. The cast of *Bold Women*, *The Only Way is Essex* etcetera, will all be there too.'

I'm supposed to be impressed and thank him but I can't bring myself to; he's getting paid very well so why should I? I also don't like him telling me what to do and what to wear; he works for me – not the other way around.

'I'll think about it,' I say. Gerald looks at me in surprise and opens his mouth to say something and then closes it again when he sees me frown.

'You should take Doe with you,' Aiden says, completely ignoring what I've said.

'Doe?' I'm surprised; I'd sort of assumed that Gerald would come.

'Yes. Doe,' he says with the look that implies I'm being thick again. 'It's the Woman of the Year awards so of course you should take a woman with you, there'll be hardly any men there.'

He's right; and Doris, sorry, Doe, will be elated although it'll be a strain for her keeping up the posh accent all night especially if there's alcohol flowing.

'And you can both write your dresses off as a business cost if you can't borrow them for free.'

Doris will love it; a fancy night out and a free outfit too; no need to refit the tags and take it back to Debenhams the next day.

'Hmm..' I twirl the stem of my water glass around thoughtfully. 'Like I said, I'll think about it.'

'Let me know. I'll hold the tickets until tomorrow morning and if I don't hear from you I'll offer them to one of my other clients.' Aiden doesn't exactly snap but I know that I've rattled him because I can see the slightest tinge of pink in his cheeks and an *almost* frown.

'I'll let you know in the morning.' I smile sweetly.

I'll text him first thing in the morning to say I'm going because I don't want him giving the tickets away to anyone else because there's no way on earth I'd miss it and with Doris coming it'll be good fun.

But let Aiden wait.

He needs to know who's boss.

My cod and chips were delicious and I feel quite virtuous because although they're not part of *The*

Travis Way, they are *normal* food, not binge food. And I only had one bar of chocolate for dessert, even if it was a family size one – which is good going considering I've hardly eaten since my binge on Monday night.

My binge food of choice is basically anything in a packet that requires nil preparation apart from opening the packet and shovelling it in; crisps, cakes, chocolate bars and biscuits are just a few such foods although if I'm desperate pretty much anything will do. If I'm full on binging I don't bother with having a meal first because it's just a waste of calories.

I could easily binge right now even though I've already eaten but I have no other food in the house, not even a slice of cheese. There are tins of tomatoes and other canned goods in the cupboard but I won't bother with them – there are limits to what I'll binge on. I could put on my glasses and headscarf disguise and go out and buy something but I'm not that desperate so I'm going to go without; I feel quite virtuous.

Maybe I'll just finish this bottle of wine instead.

Ping!

A WhatsApp message lights up my phone and I pick it up with disinterest; I have few friends so I know that it's either Gerald, Doris or possibly Aiden, who is most definitely *not* a friend and just wants to nag at me and tell me what to do.

I stare at the message for several minutes trying to make sense of it and I have to reread it several times before it sinks in and makes sense.

Hi doll hows it going saw you on telly and you looked well hot you must be minted with your book and stuff im good but had a bit of bother with the old jalopy gonna cost over a grand to fix ☹ wanna hook up

The lack of any type of punctuation and the fact that he's called me *doll* means that it can only be one person; Blake. He obviously still has my number even though I deleted his.

What the hell does he want – why has he contacted me and why does he think I would possibly care about his car?

Who knows? I don't care what he wants, I decide, and I definitely do not want to meet up with him. I'm about to delete his message but stop myself; there's something bothering me about it and I can't put my finger on what it is. I decide to keep the message so that I can look at it when I haven't drunk three quarters of a bottle of wine.

I put the phone on the table and pick up my glass.

Blake?

Blake was my secret lover.

Well I did say I hadn't been celibate, didn't I?

CHAPTER FOUR

Doris should be arriving shortly; we're going to get ready for the Woman of The Year Awards together. Doris informed me that she'd be coming to my apartment at four o'clock with a bottle of wine and her dress, shoes and make-up kit and we could spend the next couple of hours tarting ourselves up and getting the party started with a glass of wine or three.

She announced this as if it was a perfectly normal way to behave and I nodded dumbly, and smiled, and agreed that it would be *fab*.

It might be; I have no idea because I've never done it before – it's one of the many things I've never done in my sheltered, abnormal life. Mother would never tolerate alcohol in the house let alone other people coming over to get ready for a night out.

Not that I'll be telling Doris that; I don't want her to think I'm a complete loser and she also believes that Mother was a sweet little old lady so I don't want to look like a liar, either.

I was going to put a few bowls of crisps and peanuts on the table to go with the wine but quickly ditched that idea because I've barely eaten since yesterday morning so that I'll look super slim at the awards. If I start eating now I won't be able to stop and I'll end up hoovering up everything in sight. I'll have to go easy on the wine too; empty stomach and all that.

Doris and I have been loaned dresses from an up and coming designer whose full name I forget; most probably because I wasn't really listening when she told me. Juliet something or other, willowy and wafer thin with masses of bright red frizzy hair resembling an enormous halo around her head. She put me in mind of an excitable red setter – she waved her arms around exuberantly every time she spoke and each word was emphasised with a different arm movement which made the assorted bangles on her arms jingle up and down as they raced from the top of her skinny arms down to her wrists. She called everyone *darling* which I found strange because we'd only just met, but maybe she does that because she can't remember people's names. She was also ultra posh and I felt like a yokel on a day out from the farm and I notice that Doris hardly said a word either so I think she was feeling the same.

We weren't given a choice about the dresses we'd like to borrow as she'd already decided what dresses we were going to wear before we even got there. I have to admit to being a bit disappointed and if she wasn't lending them to us for free I would have complained. Doris's dress is much nicer than mine – it's a long, shimmering gold number with a glittery, swishy, fish tail and she looks absolutely amazing in it; a petite, blonde, glamorous mermaid.

Mine is a rather dull pale grey affair, a very simple floor length tube dress with a scooped neck at the front and a back so low that I had to buy a special bra contraption to wear underneath it. I've seen very similar dresses to it in the prom department in Debenhams but I'm guessing that this one doesn't come with a Debenhams price tag. The disappointment must have shown on my face because Juliet started prattling on about *less is more* and *gilding the lily* and rubbish like that and I didn't bother making a fuss about me being the star and not Doris because it all seemed like too much effort and it wouldn't have made me look very good, would it? I'd have looked like a petulant madam with an overinflated opinion of myself, which I'm really not; it's just that *I* was the one invited to the awards and Doris is the *plus one.* I'm going to look like the plus one; the plain Jane companion to Doris's glamorous mermaid.

I'm really not conceited; I have many faults that I'm only too aware of, the main ones being that I'm an accomplished liar and an attempted murderer (by accident), but I don't think I'm vain or self-important and even when I lie it's only when I absolutely have to.

Or when I'm bored.

But I'm trying not to do that. Honestly.

Anyway, realistically no-one is even going to notice me with all of the other well known celebrities there so it doesn't really matter who looks the best because the paparazzi are hardly going to be interested in some ex-fattie from nowhere land who's written a boring diet book.

The doorbell rings at the exact moment that my phone pings and as I head to the front door to let Doris in I glance at my phone to see that Blake has sent me another message. I can't think why he's started pestering me but I won't allow him to spoil my night out.

* * *

I don't think Doris has drawn breath since she got here; she's been to my apartment once before but it wasn't for any length of time. It was just after I'd moved in and she called in on her way into town on a night out with a pot plant (now dead) and a *Happy New Home* card. I gave her a quick guided tour and she went on her way and didn't seem particularly interested at the time because she was in a bit of a rush to meet up with her low rent friends.

Now she seems mega interested; she's talking about wanting to get her own place as she's fed up with living with her parents but I know that really she's angling to move in here with me because she's mentioned my two spare bedrooms at least three times. I'm making non-committal sounds between sips of wine because there's no way I want her moving in with me. My secret eating would be discovered in no time at all and the lie of my diet book would be out and there's no way I could cope with having a secret life in my very own apartment. I could hardly lock Doris in her bedroom like I did with Mother, could I? I have to have some freedom even if it is only behind the walls of my own home.

No. It's not going to happen and anyway, I'm paying her a very good salary so she could afford to rent a nice place of her own if she cut down on the cigarettes and nights out. She's also far too untidy and I do like to live in an orderly fashion – she's been here less than an hour and my lounge already looks as if it's been burgled.

Although a small part of me almost wanted to say *yes, move in,* because sometimes it would be nice to have some company and she *is* very funny and she does make me laugh. The evenings can stretch very long and lonely and I wish I didn't have to live this secret eating life because it's absolutely no fun at all, not even while I'm doing it; it's exhausting.

It's a compulsion; I *have* to do it because if I've starved myself for several days don't I deserve to eat and eat until I feel sick? Isn't that my reward and the whole point of it? This is the skewed relationship I have with food; it's almost as if I'm at war with myself and binging often feels more like a punishment than a pleasure but I don't seem to be able to stop myself.

I've even considered taking up smoking to get myself out of the cycle of binge, starve, crave and binge again because I noticed that Doris stays slim without any effort at all. She never finishes a meal because she's always in a hurry to get outside and light up a fag. I made it my mission to go outside with her when she wanted a cigarette to find out if it would work for me but I had to abandon the idea of smoking quite quickly because I couldn't stop coughing. It wasn't as if I'd even attempted to smoke a cigarette, I was only standing next to her.

It's lucky that she hinted at moving in before the wine properly took hold otherwise I think she might have been able to talk me into it.

We're on our second glasses of wine and Doris has put the heated rollers in my hair that she brought with her – they're her mum's apparently – I don't know quite how she managed to fit them all on my head and they burned my scalp a bit when she put them in but they've cooled off now. We're sitting in front of the dressing table mirror and I have my dressing gown on and Doris is wearing a silver set of matching bra and briefs which looks more like a bikini. As she applies the last of my make-up I notice how tanned and glowing she is - as if she's just got back from a week in the Med.

By comparison I'm going to look pasty and washed out in that boring grey dress. I wish I'd had the forethought to get myself a spray tan like Doris but it never even crossed my mind. I might as well put a pair of glasses on and carry a book because I'm going to look as if I've just left the library.

We're going to put our dresses on *before* we apply our lipstick because I don't think Juliet will want her designer dresses returned with *Screaming Siren* splattered all over them.

'There, I fink that's perfect. I'll just whip these rollers out and we can get our frocks on and I'll do the lippy.'

I wince as she rips the rollers from my head with a good bit of my hair still attached to them and I watch in the mirror as she fluffs my hair with her tiny hands and squirts nearly the entire contents of a can of hairspray on it.

'There, what do you fink?'

I'm both horrified and enthralled by my reflection; I never knew Doris had such a gift for putting make-up on although I should have realised because since she had her transformation I've never seen her without a full face of the stuff.

She's darkened my normally non-descript eyebrows with pencil and brushed smoky grey eye shadow over my eyelids, making my eyes appear huge. I turn my face this way and that to scrutinise the foundation she's applied so carefully; she's done a very good job and my skin looks porcelain-like with no sign of a blemish. My hair is a jumble of waves and curls which Doris assures me will not drop despite me telling her that usually by the time I've walked outside to the car any hint of wave will have vanished. I gently stroke my hand over my hair to find that it feels as rigid as cement, it's as if I'm touching a cycling helmet made of hair.

'You don't think it's a bit much?' I ask as I gaze at myself. Do I look slightly drag queenish? The Screaming Siren lipstick that is yet to be applied is a pillar box red and I wonder if it'll all look a bit too much. Especially as I look like a ghost next to Doris's bronzed body.

'Na, course not. If you don't have loads on you'll look proper washed out under the cameras and you won't 'ave a face.' She picks up the blusher and brushes a bit more onto my cheeks and I wonder if she deliberately didn't tell me she was getting a fake tan so that she'd look better than me.

I dismiss the thought immediately and tell myself not to be so uncharitable; it's probably completely normal behaviour for a night out but I wouldn't know because I never go anywhere.

It doesn't really matter anyway because I don't think we're going to have any cameras pointing our way but I don't want to spoil it for Doris by telling her that so I smile sweetly.

'Okay, if you're sure.'

'I am. Now help me into my dress and then you can get yours on. I fink we'd better get a move on 'cos the taxi's gonna be here soon.'

I glance at the clock and see to my horror that

we only have ten minutes to finish getting dressed. I hurriedly swallow down the rest of my glass of wine and Doris does the same.

'And don't forget.' Doris drops her glass down on the dressing table with a bang. 'To call me Doe when we're there. Don't want people finking I'm fucking common.'

* * *

The taxi isn't a taxi at all but a limousine and Doris and I languish on the back seat as if we're two film stars. It's just over an hour's drive to London and we're both sitting with our legs stretched out straight in front of us so that we don't crease our dresses. Our shoes are off and neatly arranged in front of the doors ready to put on when we arrive at the awards.

'You look fab, wish I had that dress.' Doris turns her head to appraise me.

'Really? Let's swap then, because I'd much rather have yours. This would look better with a tan. You can lend me your bra as well.'

Doris ponders this for a moment and then shakes her head.

'Na, better not. I don't fink my bra would fit you and to be honest I don't fancy my tits swinging around loose wiv all them cameras about.'

I don't much fancy mine swinging about either but I don't have a lot of choice. I curse Juliet and her stupid dress; why did she have to lend me a dress that I can't wear normal underwear with? The dress material is so silky and smooth that it showed every strap and bump of the stupid bra contraption that I bought. I struggled putting it on and wrapping the extra long straps around my waist and I had to keep looking at the packet it came in to make sure I'd done it up correctly. Then when I put this awful dowdy dress on and looked in the mirror I could see that every strap and hook was clearly visible through the material. I briefly considered wearing a different dress but despite my wardrobes being full of unworn designer outfits there was nothing at all in them suitable for the Women of the Year awards. I don't have anything floor length or glamorous enough because I never *go* anywhere glamorous.

In a fit of temper I took the dress off, ripped the bra off and flung it into the corner of the room and then pulled the dress back on without a bra. All in front of Doris too, because I was in such a rage and I'd drunk too much wine and I knew that the driver was impatiently waiting outside my apartment ready to leave because he kept honking his horn.

I could kill Juliet. I think I might accidentally on purpose smear lipstick all over this awful dress before I give it back to her.

Even the outline of my knickers showed through the dress and I had to search through my chest of drawers until I found a barely there thong which I'd bought ages ago and never worn. Thank

God I found it otherwise I'd be knicker-less too although the thong is so tiny that it barely covers the essentials.

'Aiden done well getting us such a lush car didn't he?' Doris strokes the brushed suede seat with her fingers. 'I ain't never been in nuffink like this before.'

I haven't either but I shrug as if I do it all of the time. I'm annoyed that he ordered it without asking because I'm paying for it so he should have consulted me first; although I suppose it would have looked a bit odd if we'd arrived in a battered *Frogham Cars* taxicab.

'We could crack open that champagne.' Doris nods her head in the direction of the fully stocked bar in front of her. 'Have a little drinkie before we get there.'

I'm about to say no and then think *sod it*, I'm paying for it all so why not? I'm surprised that Aiden didn't have all of the alcohol removed from the car before it arrived to pick us up, he's such a control freak. When I texted him yesterday morning to say that Doris and I would be attending the awards he replied with an extremely long and boring text informing me of the correct behaviour for the event. He also sent a very similar text to Doris just in case I'd forgotten how to read. She glanced at it and promptly deleted it, which is what I should have done. The gist of it was:

No alcohol.

No answering any questions about my private

life (as if anyone would be remotely interested and who's going to ask and I don't have a private life anyway).

No alcohol.

No alcohol.

He re-iterated the no alcohol bit over and over and said it had ruined many a would-be celebrity's career before it had even started. Apparently the very worst thing that could happen would be pictures of me in all of the newspapers clambering into the limousine at the end of the night with mascara running down my face and my shoes and knickers in my hand.

Okay, he didn't say that about the mascara, knickers and shoes but the text was so unbelievably tedious and boring that I had to spice it up somehow. He'd probably have a heart attack if he knew we'd already drunk one bottle of wine before we'd even left my apartment.

'Yeah, let's go for it.' I say as I lean forward and pull the bottle from the rack. 'Grab those two glasses.'

* * *

I feel decidedly unsteady as I get out of the limousine and I make a conscious effort to straighten up and walk very carefully and slowly onto the square in front of the awards building. The teetering silver heels that I know will have rubbed my feet red raw by the end of the night might look gorgeous but they're extremely tricky to walk in. Doris follows behind me and grabs hold of my hand to pull me back to wait for her.

'You okay?' She's looking up at me with huge, round eyes and I think that we definitely shouldn't have drunk so much on an empty stomach.

'Are you feeling a bit drunk as well?' I lean down and whisper in her ear. I must say I'm a bit surprised because I thought she was a hardened drinker as she's always going out clubbing with her various rough friends.

She covers her mouth to stifle a laugh.

'Course not! We've hardly had anyfing,' she whispers. 'It's all these people looking at us, I didn't fink there'd be this many.'

And that's when I glance around whilst trying to maintain my balance on the heels; she's not wrong, there are what seem like *hundreds* of people standing on the pavement on either side of the venue, held at bay by chunky ropes on gold coloured stands. Not just women but men too and even some children; the throng of people stretches back down the street and I realise that I never noticed them as we drove up to the exhibition centre because I was staring at my feet. I was starting to feel a bit car sick with the alcohol and lack of food and was taking deep breaths to calm myself. Thank God we get a meal before they present the awards; I need some food to soak up the alcohol.

'Look! That's 'er out of TOWIE, look at her lips! She looks like a trout,' Doris whispers excitedly.

I follow Doris's gaze to see a mahogany tanned blond wearing a miniscule chain mail mini dress pouting and posing for a gaggle of photographers outside the open doors to the venue. With her hands on her hips she turns this way and that and then gives a final flick of her long blonde hair before she glides slowly through the doorway into the foyer. I watch and admire her professionalism; if I attempted to flick my hair like that I'd definitely fall over; not that I could flick my hair, it's so rigid that if Doris got in the way I could probably knock her out. As she disappears from view the photographers turn as one to look over at the new arrivals.

Us.

'GO ON! Put yer best sexy walk on,' Doris hisses in my ear and she gives me a little shove in the back as she lets go of my hand.

Like a rabbit caught in the headlights I walk slowly and carefully towards the doorway and I'm aware of Doris strutting confidently beside me. Regretting drinking all of that wine and champagne, I concentrate on not falling over and reaching the safety of the exhibition centre so that I can sit down and recover and ease the torturous shoes off my feet.

A grubby looking man pops up in front of me and shouts in my face.

'Alison! This way!' A camera is shoved towards

me and I freeze. Everyone seems to be calling my name but I stand immobile; I can't seem to move but I'm aware of Doris next to me pouting and posing. I find myself staring around helplessly at the crowd and wish it would end. After what feels like several hours of this I feel Doris's hand on my back again and I'm propelled towards the door and into the building.

* * *

I knew the room would be big because they have car and boat exhibitions here but I'm still shocked by the size of it; it's enormous and filled with what seems like hundreds of white table-clothed round tables. Each table has a centrepiece of pink and white roses which look real but could be fake for all I know, sparkling crystal glasses and shiny silver cutlery to complete the look. Each chair is shrouded in pink chiffon topped off with a huge pink bow tied at the back. It's quite a sight to behold and I can't help but be impressed – it must certainly have taken some organising.

A short, dapper man in a pink jacket beckons us with a flick of his finger and we follow him as he takes us to our table. His jacket is a pink version of a circus ringmaster's costume and I wonder if he's going to pull a whip out from his pocket and crack it to make us walk faster. As this thought crosses my mind I realise that I really need to eat something because I've obviously had far too much to drink.

He does a smart about turn as we reach our seats and then heads back to the door to greet more guests. There are only a few people already seated at other tables and there's no-one at our table, we must be some of the first to arrive. Doris is walking around the table looking at the place names slotted into the name holders fashioned as generous cleavage popping out of shiny pink fake bras.

So much pink.

Doris deftly swaps two bras from one side of the table to the other.

'What are you doing?' I hiss.

'Getting us better seats. Won't be able to see nuffin' from these two.'

She's right; in our original seats we'd have had our backs to the stage and had to crane our necks around to see what was going on behind us.

I look at the names of the two she's swapped us with and see that's it's Jackie and Denise who are two presenters from *Bold Women*, a hugely popular daytime television talk show. Mother used to watch it occasionally just so she could call them trollops and disagree with everything that they said.

'Doris! Put them back! They've been put there because they're famous, we're not!'

Doris shrugs. 'Should've got here first then, shouldn't they?' She plonks herself down in the seat facing the stage.

I'm about to argue and then change my mind; my feet hurt and I need to sit down because my legs feel all wobbly. God knows what the photographs of me will look like; I couldn't even manage to smile because I was so nervous so I probably look like a pale, village idiot on a day out in the big smoke, which is basically what I am. Although I don't need to worry because they won't even use the photographs – Doris and I are hardly famous and lots of real celebrities have been invited.

I really shouldn't have drunk so much alcohol on an empty stomach and I don't know why I did - I've been on television twice before so it's not as if I was nervous and needed a drink. I think I only drank the champagne to spite Aiden although I'm the one paying so I don't know why I think I was getting one over on him.

I don't know why I froze outside either, stage fright, I suppose. Still, the worst is over now; I can settle back now and enjoy the meal and the awards and as the table cloth is so long I can take off these agonising stilettos. I don't need any shoes on because I'm hardly going to be going up to the stage to collect an award.

Doris and I people watch as the room slowly fills up; the eight remaining seats on our table are soon taken but apart from Jackie and Denise from *Bold Women,* I don't recognise any of the others although they all look extremely glamorous and not at all nervous. Jackie and Denise look a bit put out when they realise that they have their backs to the stage and they look pointedly at Doris and I. I open my mouth to say we'll move but Doris gives me a kick under the table so I close it again.

Considering the evening is supposed to be all about the sisterhood of women and how wonderful we are and how we all stick together, I soon realise that nobody really speaks to anyone else apart from the person they've come with. A brief *hello* to everyone else at the table, a quick scan of the other guests dresses and hair to make sure they're not being outshone and that's it. All of the guests seem to be intent on checking their make-up in their tiny handbag mirrors, whispering to their plus ones and checking their mobile phones whilst furtively eyeing up the opposition.

'I fink the foods on its way.'

I follow the direction of Doris's eyes to see more pink jacketed waiters bringing out trays of food. Thank God for that; I'm absolutely ravenous and starting to feel a bit sick. I honestly don't know how much longer I can go on with the binging and starving.

'What you 'aving? I'm going for the chicken and poncy potatoes.'

I look at Doris in surprise.

'I didn't know there was a choice.'

'Yeah course there is, Aiden texted me last night. Chicken, some crappy vegan option or a salad. He said there weren't gonna be no starters 'cos it fucks up the filming schedule or somefing like that.'

Aiden didn't text me and I can guess why. This is confirmed when a pink jacketed waiter places a large plate with a very small salad on it in front of me. He then places Doris's chicken with Duchess potatoes and vegetables in front of her.

'Don't fink much of yours,' Doris says as she picks up her knife and fork, 'You should have gone for the same as me.'

Aiden, the bastard, doesn't even trust me to choose my own meal. I would have chosen the salad anyway because I daren't eat in public but he could have done me the courtesy of allowing me to make my own decision. If he didn't make me so much money and he wasn't so good at his job I'd sack him.

Speaking of bastards reminds me; I haven't read the latest message from Blake. I pull my mobile out of my tiny handbag and open up WhatsApp.

Hey doll hows it going you I expect ure too busy to text back we should catch up soon talk about old times and the fun we had �� *id come over and see you but still not got the jalopy fixed when we gonna meet up*

I don't like the reference to the *fun we had*, something about it sounds vaguely threatening but maybe I'm being paranoid.

I am being paranoid, I decide as I put my mobile back in my clutch bag and squash it closed with difficulty and place it on the table. I pick up my knife and fork and prepare to eat the paltry food on offer when I remember something else about my arrival.

Blake.

In the sea of faces gawping at the red carpet a vision of one of them pops into my head with sudden clarity. Blake; he was amongst the crowd outside on the pavement when I arrived. Somehow he must have known that I'd be here and he was watching and waiting for me to arrive.

The fact that he came to London especially to see me is not good.

Not good at all.

CHAPTER FIVE

I met Blake when I viewed my apartment; he worked at the estate agents where it was for sale and showed me around. It wasn't Brothertons where Bella was the Sales Manager, but Shipleys, who were their major opposition. I remember being disappointed about that fact at the time because I wanted Bella to know that I had pots of money and that I was looking for a house or apartment to buy. Even though I was over my embarrassing infatuation with Bella and her life I still daydreamed about being all superior as she showed me around lots of houses that I could dismiss haughtily as not good enough.

All complete nonsense of course because when I thought about it properly I knew that I needed to keep my distance from her because of the *porn on the laptop* thing. I knew that I hadn't left a trail of evidence or anything but I also knew that if the police started looking into it in earnest they would soon find the fake email account that I'd set up which would eventually lead all too quickly to me. Thanks to Gerald the police had released me but I think if he hadn't come to my rescue I'd have caved in to the questioning. I knew that if Justin decided to take it further and find out what had really happened he'd soon put two and two together and realise that it was me. I think I was extremely lucky getting away with attempted murder and I wouldn't have been able to pull off the innocent act so successfully a second time.

When I arrived to view the apartment Blake was outside the entrance leaning against a Porsche with a bunch of keys and a cheeky smile. I could feel his eyes on me as I got out of my brand new MX5 and I did put on a bit of a wiggle as I sashayed towards him. I remember feeling slightly impressed that he had a Porsche and reasoned that he must sell an awful lot of houses to afford a car like that.

Blake has the sort of flashy good looks that are very attractive for a short period of time but then begin to fade quite quickly when the fast food diet and lack of a good dentist start to catch up. I'm sure you've seen the type; gorgeous at twenty, attractive at thirty but pretty much done by forty when the teeth start to go and the cheap suit looks well, cheap, and by the time they're fifty they're a complete embarrassment because they don't realise that they no longer have *it* but continue trying to crack onto women half their age. Blake is a couple of years older than me so he's still hanging on by a thread - floppy sun streaked, surfer dude hair and a lopsided, sexy smile finished off with what I thought was a cockney accent - although I later discovered he came from Portsmouth, or Pompey as he called it. I also found out quite quickly that the Porsche wasn't his either, he'd *borrowed* it from a friend although the friend didn't seem to know that Blake had borrowed it and he had to do a lot of grovelling to avoid being charged.

So there he was, cocksure and showing off in his borrowed/stolen Porsche and he made no secret of the fact that he fancied me rotten; made no attempt to hide his eyes travelling up and down my body and I must admit that I was flattered because it's nice to be admired. In the time it took him to insert the key in the lock and open the front door, with a few innocent estate agent-like questions he'd established that I was single and buying the apartment for myself.

As soon as I stepped inside the hallway of the apartment I knew that it was everything that I'd ever wanted and I *had* to have it so he didn't even have to sell it to me. Brand, spanking new with a faint smell of paint and new carpets (neutral colours and expensive), the spacious hallway and huge lounge with large picture windows were everything that the house at Duck Pond Lane wasn't. A state of the art kitchen with smooth white, glossy cupboard doors and pale beech worktops were a million miles away from the god-awful seventies throwback of Mother's kitchen. I wandered around in a trance and marvelled at the fact that I could easily afford this huge apartment and have lots of money to spare as well. In my mind's eye I was already furnishing the rooms with all of the things that I'd previously never been able to have and if I could have moved in that day, I would.

To be honest I didn't take too much notice of Blake after the initial *hello* because I was so taken with the apartment it was all I could think about and concentrate on and Blake barely registered. I also wasn't looking for a relationship at all – that space was firmly reserved for Gerald at some unspecified date in the distant future.

When I got around to it.

After I'd finished the viewing I drove off and forgot all about Blake and that was it as far as I was concerned; I wasn't sufficiently interested in him to take it any further. He did attempt to ask me out before I left but I pretended that I didn't know what he was talking about, played it a bit thick, I suppose, because I really couldn't be bothered although a part of me acknowledged that he was quite attractive in a ropey sort of way.

Whilst the purchase of the apartment was going through Blake rang me at every opportunity on totally trivial matters and if I hadn't been so keen for the sale to go through and move, I probably wouldn't have even answered his calls. I found him sort of attractive but had absolutely no intention of going out with him – as I've said I was saving myself for Gerald and really, apart from Gerald's *going on*, Gerald doesn't really have any faults and Blake didn't come close to him in any way. Blake was nice enough and reasonably good looking but he didn't have Gerald's class and I just wasn't interested. I was excitedly ordering furniture so that as soon as the sale completed I could have it all delivered and move in straight away. I found that shops were very accommodating on delivery dates when money is no object.

And I would never have seen Blake again and I gave him no thought at all until he turned up unannounced at my front door a couple of weeks after I'd moved in. He caught me at a weak moment; the first flush of excitement at having my lovely new flat was starting to wear off and I felt a bit lonely, I suppose. I had all of this new found freedom and money and I didn't really know what to do with it. It wasn't that I missed Mother or anything weird like that, it was just strange having only myself to worry about and not having to look after and consider someone else all of the time. I could please myself totally and it somehow felt wrong, as if something was missing. The few months while the sale was going through on the house had been taken up with getting rid of all that dreadful old tatty furniture and clearing out Duck Pond Lane; not to mention finding somewhere to invest all of Mother's money.

Probate had taken quite a while because she

had even more money than I knew about; apart from the online accounts that I had access to she had investment bonds, a portfolio of shares that turned out to be worth an awful lot and the maximum amount of premium bonds allowed. For a while I couldn't figure out how she'd kept it all from me because I never saw a thing in the post that came to the house. It transpired that Mother had her very own financial advisor that she used to telephone every week, most likely when I was at work. He was instructed not to send details of her investments by letter but to speak to her on the phone only, which must have been tricky for her once I'd cut her phone off.

I was astonished at the extent of Mother's duplicity; I knew she was a liar but I still couldn't quite believe that she'd amassed so much money without me knowing. There was also the fact that if I hadn't gone through the boxes of letters and files in the loft before throwing them out would I have ever known? I suppose her secret financial advisor would have eventually contacted the police when he was unable to contact her, but who knows how long that might have taken. Gerald dealt with Probate and sorted everything out for me but I had to go through every piece of paper in that house to make that I didn't miss any other hidden investments or accounts. The only downside was that I had to pay tax on my inheritance because there was so much of it but I can't really grumble because there was just *so* much money.

So much, in fact, that I didn't really need to sell the house at all to buy my apartment. But it had to go; I hated that house and all of the rotten memories associated with it and I wanted no further tie to it. I did consider just walking away and getting a house clearance firm to clear the lot – Mothers personal effects, my old clothes, everything so that I wouldn't have to look at any of it ever again because there wasn't one thing in there that I intended keeping. The only thing that stopped me was the thought that Mother had made a will leaving everything to the local cat's home or something similar and hidden it somewhere, because I wouldn't have put it past her. So aside from looking for hidden investments I was also looking for a will made in spite. I had to ensure that someone else didn't find it first and I'd end up with nothing.

So I went through every single item in that house, just to be sure that she hadn't, and I think that took it out of me, going through all of the years of accumulated stuff because it was like reliving my childhood all over again – and not in a good way. The cellar was the worst but I couldn't leave it because that's just the place where she would have hidden something because she knew I hated it down there and avoided it at all costs.

I never did find a will but if I had it would have gone straight into the shredder. It crossed my mind that she could have made a will and lodged it with a solicitor and then what could I do? But as time went on and nothing happened I started to breathe a bit easier; I told myself that if the worse happened Gerald would sort it out because he is very good at his job.

After I'd been through the entire house I burned all of the family photographs and the contents of Mother's dresser because what was the point of keeping any of it? I made a nice big bonfire in the middle of the garden inside an old oil drum that was lurking behind the shed and I set fire to the lot. I think I hoped it would make me feel better, be cathartic, but it didn't.

I just felt sad.

And angry; because all of those years when I was a child and she'd never bought me so much as a toy and never let me go on the school trips because *she couldn't afford it* were complete lies. All the years she told me that we couldn't afford a holiday and the way she took my cleaning wages off me made me hate her even more because things could have been so different; I could have been so different. If she hadn't been so warped we could have had a good life and I struggled to understand why she was so spiteful and full of hate for me.

Anyway, all of this is the background to the reason for falling into bed with Blake so easily and basically it's all Mother's fault as well as my own. When he called round that evening I remember that I only answered the door because I thought it might have been Gerald - because apart from Doris

I have no other friends – and I was surprised when I opened my glossy new front door to find Blake clutching a bottle of prosecco and a wilting bunch of cheap garage bought flowers.

I know that I need to make some more friends but it's difficult because most people have friends from school or they make friends at their place of work and I don't work so perhaps that's another reason to get a job. Also, I think people would see straight through me and see that I'm not a very nice person (although I do keep trying) and that really I'm shaping up to be just like Mother. I honestly wonder how long it'll take Gerald and Doris to see what I'm really like and I'm surprised that realisation hasn't dawned already.

So, there he was, with his cocky smile, and it took me a moment to recognise him without his work suit on (incidentally, no-one compares favourably to Gerald in a suit) and he did look a lot more attractive in faded, raggy jeans and a pale pink linen shirt. Even so I was going to be really ungracious and take the offered bottle of prosecco and flowers from him and shut the door on him but he lolled against the door frame casually which prevented me from shutting it. He then sweet talked and flattered me so much that it would have felt churlish not to let him in.

Once inside he insisted that I show him around the apartment and in every room he congratulated me on how good it was looking with my new furnishings and what a transformation I'd achieved.

Once I'd show him all of the rooms we returned to the lounge and had an awkward few minutes where we stood silently and I think he was waiting for me to offer him a drink – which I had absolutely no intention of doing. Eventually he got fed up with waiting and picked up the bottle of wine from the coffee table where I'd left it and waved it around and said *how about opening it and having a toast to your new home*. What could I say, I could hardly refuse could I? So begrudgingly I went out to the kitchen and returned with two of my lovely new wine glasses and we sat down on the sofa.

Just one glass to be polite, I thought, and then I can send him on his way. Blake opened the wine and poured us both a glass and after a while I started to enjoy myself. Blake is funny in a wide boy, *Del Trotterish* sort of way and the fact that he blatantly fancied me helped too. He was flattering me outrageously, telling me that I was the most beautiful woman he'd ever met and that he remembered our first meeting and had been dreaming of seeing me again. What can I say? I'm only human.

When we'd drunk all of the prosecco – and actually, I think I drank most of it because he was very clever and kept topping me up – we opened a bottle of red that I had in my brand new wine rack in the kitchen. The wine made me feel better, more relaxed, more normal. It was inevitable really; we ended up in bed together and he didn't even have to try very hard; I was there for the taking.

I regret it now, of course, and I wish that I'd just given in to Gerald on the many occasions when he made it quite plain that he desperately wanted me but the thing is, one of the reasons I kept putting Gerald off was that I was sure he'd soon get bored of me. Because I hadn't had much of a sex life, you see, and I was terrified that he'd think I was some sort of sad reborn virgin and that the whole experience would be humiliating - because he's obviously had lots of stunning girlfriends and been around the block. I'd only had one boyfriend when I was eighteen and we'd only slept together twice and then Mother had her stroke and that was the end of that. So you could say that Blake was practice really. For Gerald. Although I'm pretty sure Gerald wouldn't see it that way.

Anyway, the whole Blake thing wouldn't have been so bad if that had been it but we continued our little affair for nearly three months. I know; I can scarcely believe it myself. I kept telling him that I wasn't ready for a relationship and he'd say he understood but then he'd arrive at my door a week later and somehow we'd end up in bed again. I did make sure that we never went out together anywhere because frankly I didn't want to be seen with him and I certainly didn't want Gerald to find out; the very thought was enough to make me break out into a cold sweat. And if Blake hadn't kept coming around *I* certainly wouldn't have bothered getting in touch with *him*; I'd gone off him quite quickly and he had a bit too much of a lackadaisical attitude to bodily hygiene for my liking. A couple of times he had the most awful bad breath and I had to mouth breathe when he got close to me. There was also a definite whiff of *Febreze* around his pink shirt and tattered jeans which seemed to be the only off duty outfit he possessed as he always wore it. Gerald, on the other hand, always smells gorgeous – expensive cologne and minty fresh breath and his clothes are always tip top; I know for a fact that he sends his shirts out to be laundered and he has so many suits that I scarcely see the same one twice.

I shudder now at the memory, to be honest, and my only excuse is that I was lonely and had probably gone a bit mental after all that had happened with Mother.

It all came to an end one evening when Blake announced as we lay side by side in bed, post sex, that we needed to *make things official* and hinted about moving in with me. I was shocked and absolutely horrified and it suddenly dawned on me what I'd got myself into. I didn't say anything to him but I made my mind up there and then; he had to go.

I waited for a few days and then I sent him a message on WhatsApp saying that I'd been giving it a lot of thought and I didn't want to see him anymore. He ignored it of course because I'd told him this many times and he turned up a few nights later with a bottle of cheap plonk like he usually did but this time I wouldn't let him in. He didn't like it very much and eventually went away but came back a couple of nights later because he thought he could sweet talk his way in like he always had before. This time I kept the chain on the door and talked to him through the two-inch gap. He could have easily given the door a good shove and broken the chain but I don't think he's the violent type although he got quite verbally abusive, said that I didn't get to decide when it was over, he did. His language was pretty ripe too; although I'm used to Doris so that didn't faze me much. I just let him rant and kept my mouth shut until he wore himself out and went away.

He came around again the next evening – so cocksure of his charm and my weakness – but I didn't fancy a repeat of the previous evening so I didn't even answer the door even though he kept his finger on the doorbell for ages and hammered on the door with what sounded like his fist. He eventually gave up and sent me lots of pestering WhatsApp messages – which is when I told him that if he didn't stop pestering me I'd make a complaint to his boss and then the police if he continued. That seemed to do the trick and until he texted me the other day, I hadn't heard from him for a couple of months.

I don't flatter myself that he was in love with me or anything like that – I think he loved the flat and fancied moving in and living here rent free but there was no way I was going to let that happen.

He was always a bit vague about where he lived and tried to give the impression that he shared a flat *with the boys* but I think he did his fair bit of sofa surfing because the lack of personal hygiene and the *Febrezed* clothing were a bit of a giveaway.

So. Now he's texted me twice and I wonder what he's up to – he obviously wants something and the fact that he's mentioned his old banger of a car in each text suggests that he's after money though why he thinks I'd be interested in his financial situation I don't know.

But it's bothering me; he's texted me and he was loitering outside the *Women of the Year* awards last night. I suppose I'll have to reply to him to find out what he wants; maybe I'll have to threaten to report him to his boss again if he keeps pestering. I pick my phone up and compose a WhatsApp message to him, trying to keep it as neutral as possible. After half an hour of faffing around and deleting it and then retyping it I finally decide that blunt and to the point is the way to go – I don't want to give him even the tiniest suggestion that there's any chance of him getting back with me. He's so cocky he probably thinks that if I meet up with him we'll fall into bed again because I won't be able to resist his grubby charm.

No chance, I have too much to lose and I don't trust him and I just wish I'd not been such a fool to fall for it the first time.

What do you want? I type, *Why do you want to meet?*

Can't get much blunter than that, can I? He surely can't read anything into that. My finger hovers for a moment and then I hit the *send* button; I just need to get it over with, find out what he wants and get rid.

Thank God I never went out anywhere in public with him and no one even knows that we were *sort* of together; God, the humiliation if anyone ever found out. Thank God Gerald has no idea.

It's such a shame that Blake doesn't have a peanut allergy.

Only joking.

Sort of.

* * *

'AL!' I hold the phone away from my ear to prevent Doris's excitable screaming from bursting my eardrum.

'You seen the papers?'

The papers? Does she mean the newspapers because if she does, I haven't, and I'm surprised if Doris has because she doesn't strike me as the reading type, if you know what I mean. I haven't even got up yet; I'm still languishing in bed mulling over the Blake situation. When my phone rang, for one horrible moment I was sure it was him.

'No I haven't. I don't get newspapers delivered.'

Doris tuts. 'Na, I mean online. You're in all of

them, all over 'em.'

My first thought is Blake; has he tired of waiting for me to reply and sold his story to one of the gutter tabloids? I dismiss this thought immediately; he has no story and more to the point, no proof because I made quite sure that he never took any selfies of the two of us although he was always trying. I always put my hand up in front of my face or turned my head away and it used to annoy him intensely and he'd ask if I was ashamed of him. Obviously, I was, but I'd say of course not but that I hated having my photograph taken without make-up on because I never bothered putting make-up on just for him. I don't think he believed me but he never pushed it because he didn't want to start an argument as he was buttering me up so that he could move in.

'Nooo...'

'Fucks sake, Al, get wiv it. Go online and 'ave a look, you're famous. I'm coming over so we can look properly on your laptop, can't see very well on me phone. See you in an hour.'

Without waiting for a reply Doris rings off and I stare at the phone like an idiot.

I quickly type *The Sun* into the tiny browser on my phone followed by my name. I squint at the story and photographs on the tiny screen.

Oh. My. God.

CHAPTER SIX

'There's more pictures of you than the big blonde one out of TOWIE.'

Doris and I are sitting next to each other on the sofa hunched over my laptop; I'd barely got out of the shower and got dressed before Doris arrived. I had to shampoo my hair twice to get all the hairspray out and unbelievably the curls had survived a night of sleeping on them – although the whole of my hair was lopsided and flat giving me the appearance of skew whiff Marge Simpson, although it wasn't blue of course.

When I opened the front door Doris marched straight past me and continued out to the kitchen where she yanked open the fridge and stood staring into it; she said she was starving and was going to cook us both a bacon sandwich before we started looking at the papers. She was shocked to find nothing in the fridge apart from a tub of low-fat spread and a carton of milk. She then proceeded to rifle through the cupboards and couldn't believe that I didn't have any food in the house. *What do you live on?* she demanded. I told her that I'd been busy all week and intended doing a big shop this afternoon – which I am in a way because as soon as she's gone I'll be going to the big Tesco's and buying lots of binge food. I can use the self-service till as well so I won't have a nosey cashier looking at what I'm buying and then I can come home and eat it all. I just hope Doris doesn't stay too long because the big Tesco's closes at four today.

She looked at me in disbelief and said she'd go and get us both a *Maccy D* breakfast but I stopped her and told her that I don't eat junk food. I managed to keep a straight face while I said it too; I love MacDonald's but I don't need a witness to my binging because I'm so hungry I don't think I could control myself in front of her and I'd most likely fall on a breakfast McMuffin like a ravenous wolf. She said okay and that she'd go there on her way home but she wasn't happy, she said that if she passed out from hunger it would be all my fault

'Look!' She taps the screen which is already full of her smudged finger marks. 'You're a proper celeb!'

I still can't quite believe that there are so many pictures of me in the newspapers; when the cameras were pointed at us as we arrived for the awards I felt sure the resulting photographs would be swiftly consigned to the bin and would never see the light of day again. We're both nobodies and there were lots of other celebrities there so I can only assume that it must be an extremely slow news day.

'Look, there's my 'and - you can see me silver nail varnish.'

I look closer at the screen and sure enough I can just about make out Doris's bronzed arm and tiny hand in the picture although her body has been cut off.

'I don't really understand why they've cut you out because you looked far more glamorous than I did in that awful grey dress.'

Doris turns her head and looks at me, rolls her eyes and tuts.

'You ain't 'alf fick sometimes. You look *different* from the rest of us which is why they picked you out.'

Different? I'm not super fat anymore so I'm not sure what she means. I stare at her blankly and she sighs theatrically but I can tell she's pleased that she knows something that I don't.

'You look pale and stuck up; not orange and fake like the rest of us, *that's* why. I expect the papers are fed up with printing the same old crap about the same old celebs and people get fed up with reading about them. I fink that's why they make stuff up about 'em 'cos they're dead boring really.'

I think she's right although I don't know that I like being described as stuck up but I look at the pictures with new eyes; it's true that I don't have a fake tan and I'm not pouting or posing and while I felt sure that I looked like a frightened rabbit caught in a car's headlights, the very fact that I'm ghostly white and unsmiling has made me stand out from the crowd.

'See.' Doris taps the screen with her silver tipped finger. 'Apart from that bloke what won you've got the most pictures out of everyone.'

When Doris refers to *That bloke what won* she is of course referring to the winner of the Woman of the Year award. There were lots of runners up sub categories such as *most inspiring woman* and *most successful woman* because it would have been a very dull evening indeed if there'd been only one winner. They also needed to fill two hours of prime-time television so all in all I think there were ten categories with a winner for each although they began to blur after a while as did the acceptance speeches. After all of the runners up had been presented with their awards the final award was for *the* woman of the year.

Doris tips her head back and taps her teeth with her finger.

'I still don't get it.'

'Get what?'

'How a bloke can win the Woman of the Year award.'

This is a very good question and I attempt once more to explain to Doris the reasoning behind it; I tried last night but had to give up and start clapping and smiling when the cameraman swung his lens in our direction as the Woman of the Year collected his award. Their award.

'Neville Wright is exercising their right to remain gender neutral and non-binary and to dress in whatever clothes they choose. The Woman of The Year Award was awarded to them to acknowledge their bravery in choosing to act in this pioneering way whilst maintaining their current position as a BBC newsreader.' This is what it said in the newspaper that I read online this morning and I repeat it pretty much word for word.

'Why are you calling 'im they?

'Because they are non-binary and gender neutral.'

'But 'es a bloke and he's got free kids wiv his fird wife.'

'That's why they've won, because of their bravery in coming out despite difficult circumstances and previously living their life in a conformist way.'

'But 'es a bloke dressing in women's clothes, surely that's a tranny?

'He,' I start to say before correcting myself, 'They, are not a transvestite but gender neutral.'

'Na, still don't get it,' Doris says as she turns back to study the screen, 'And why would he want to win a woman's award if he's non whatsit? I mean, it makes no sense.'

I don't understand it either but I fear that we're not going to get very far in this conversation but will spend the next hour talking in circles.

'I don't know, Doris, I'm just telling you what I

read.'

'It's 'is kids I feel sorry for, they'll get it ripped out of them at school when their mates see their dad on the telly in a pink dress and high heels.'

'It's different now, everyone's more liberal and open minded.'

'Don't fink so,' Doris snorts, 'Kids ain't liberal or fair. I did like his shoes though, they were well nice even if they were a size eleven.' She starts to laugh.

'He did have big feet.' I laugh too. 'They, I mean.'

'Fucking massive,' Doris says between snorts of laughter.

For some reason we can't stop laughing and when we eventually stop we both have tears rolling down our faces.

'Anyway, enough about him, her, they, shim, whatever,' Doris says as she dabs her eyes, 'Let's look at the photos of you.' She clicks the laptop and another picture of me arriving at the awards pops up and we sit and read the article.

'Classy' is indeed the word that's being bandied around about me, mostly because I'm unsmiling and look slightly haughty as if it's all quite beneath me. The bright red *Screaming Siren* lipstick and rigid curls give me a look of someone who's stepped straight out of the nineteen fifties and I do stand out; a white figure amongst a sea of orange.

The Mail has a centre spread of the guests as they arrive at the awards but out of all of the better known celebs – apart from Neville - I'm the one they've chosen to put in the middle of the page with the headline – *Alison – who is this mystery woman?* Doris thinks it's fantastic but I feel a slight twinge of unease; what if they start digging and discover that I was arrested? What if the past comes back to haunt me? Are there laws about printing that people were arrested and released without charge? Are the newspapers allowed to print unsubstantiated gossip? Technically, I don't think they are allowed to but it doesn't usually seem to stop them.

My phone chirrups and I jump out of my skin; it's going to be Blake for sure and I suddenly don't want to know what he wants or is going to say because I'm quite certain that it's not going to be good.

'I bet those two bags from *Bold Women* hate your guts for stealing all the glory, they ain't 'ardly any pictures of them.' Doris sniggers. 'Serves 'em right for being so up their own arses.'

True, Denise and Jackie never engaged in conversation with us at all apart from a cursory *hello* when they arrived, although I noticed that when they were called up for their award – *Most Go-getting Women* - the phones which they'd been glued to since their arrival were hurriedly stuffed back into handbags before they both bestowed ear to ear beaming smiles on everyone sitting at our table as if we were all the very best of chums. Everyone smiled falsely back and applauded enthusiastically of course, because the cameras were pointing in our direction and nobody wanted to look as if they weren't happy at someone else getting an award when they hadn't, even though inside they were hating it. Not that Doris or I had any expectation of an award because we hadn't been nominated for anything and were simply there to make up the numbers; Aiden said that someone from *Tellytalk* had dropped out at the last minute due to some minor scandal.

No one else on the table spoke to us either although to be fair we never attempted to make conversation with any of them. Once we'd eaten the meal – Aiden had very nicely decided for me that I didn't want dessert so I had to watch as Doris tucked into crème brulee - I was still so hungry that I was too frightened to drink anymore after overindulging in the wine at home and the champagne in the car. Doris drank mine for me and it didn't seem to have the slightest effect on her at all whereas I'd have been unconscious and lying on the floor. She's hardened to it I presume because I can't see any sign of a hangover on her this morning either.

I sit and watch while Doris opens up screen after screen of pretty much the same picture of me and variations on the same theme – who is this mystery woman, class act, that sort of thing. I can't pretend I'm not flattered especially since it's all happened by complete accident. If I'd had a fake tan like I wished I had I'd never have been noticed. The only downside of course is that the obligatory *fat me* picture is also plastered everywhere for comparison but there's nothing I can do about that.

'Blimey, look at that blokes face, talk about creepy.' Doris hoots with laughter and points to the screen at a man in the crowd caught on camera behind me as I arrive at the awards. He stands out because the rest of the crowd are laughing and cheering but he's standing on the pavement staring at me with a serious expression on his face.

With a sinking feeling I squint and look closer; I see to my horror that it's Blake and he does indeed look extremely creepy, the surfer dude haircut looks overlong and in desperate need of a wash and he doesn't look like he's shaved in a while. Why did they have to get him in the background? I feel myself flush and in an attempt to hide my reaction I fumble for my phone to read the message.

I stare unseeing at my phone and watch out of the corner of my eye as Doris leans closer to the laptop and scrutinises the picture.

'He's looks proper creepy. I'm sure I've seen 'im before, I fink I might know 'im.'

I watch from the corner of my eye as she flicks through several screens, leaning closer and scanning the crowd in each.

'There 'e is again, he's in loads of these pictures, even the ones of the back of you. You can see 'is head's turned where he's following you with his eyes. Yuk.' She gives a shudder. 'I fink he's a bit obsessed wiv you. I fink you might have one of those prowlers here.'

I think she means stalker but I say nothing and pretend to be intent on my phone.

'I defo know 'is face.'

I feel my skin growing hotter and keep my head down while my face cools. I open the latest WhatsApp message with a sinking heart to see what Blake has replied.

'Oh for God's sake!' I shriek dramatically.

'What?' Doris looks up from the screen.

'Aiden,' I shout, holding my phone in front of her in an attempt to distract her from the laptop screen. 'He's unbelievable.'

Doris screws her eyes up and reads the message aloud.

I have arranged a meeting for this afternoon at three thirty at Langans Bar to discuss your media campaign. Please arrive promptly.

'He's such a wanker.' She laughs. 'Anyone would fink you worked for him.'

Wouldn't they just. Although at least it wasn't Blake so thank God for small mercies. But actually the fact that Blake hasn't replied is slightly freaking me out because I know that he's read the message and now I'm wondering why he hasn't answered. But at least Aiden's text has deflected Doris from the picture of Blake.

I put my phone on the table.

'Ain't you going to reply?'

'No, I'm going to ignore him, I'm fed up with him telling me what to do and demanding that I fly up to London at a moment's notice.'

'He'll only keep on texting you.'

'Don't care, I won't open them.'

'Don't blame you.' Doris turns her attention back to the screen.

I will have to reply sooner or later because he'll only keep texting and eventually ring me if I don't answer him, but I'll make him sweat for a while. I'll think I'll text Gerald and make sure he's going too, he usually does. Even a very short period of undiluted, robotic Aiden is too much to bear.

'Tell you what though.' Doris taps the screen of the laptop several times as I tap out a message to Gerald. 'I do know 'im – he used to be a mate of Charlie's. Which means he lives here in Frogham so he must of made a special journey and went all the way to London just so he could watch you walk into a featre.'

I shrug.

'Maybe he lives in London now,' I say, affecting a nonchalant reply.

Doris gives me an odd look and I can't blame her; it was a pretty lame thing to say. I should really do much better than that since I'm such an accomplished liar.

She's tapping the screen over Blake's head.

'Yeah, it's defo 'im. Blake Weaver. Charlie felt sorry for 'im and let him sleep on our sofa a few times cos he had nowhere to live. Then I got pissed off with 'im eating all our food and hanging around all the time. Fort he was God's gift, he did. I know Charlie was a bit of a wanker but at least he washed and cleaned his teef. Blake always used to stink and he wore the same clothes all the time. Didn't stop 'im getting the birds though - he always managed to get some poor saddo to drop her knickers.'

* * *

I got rid of Doris quite quickly after the text from Aiden – I told her that I had to get out of my tracksuit bottoms and tart myself up ready for our meeting. The real reason I wanted her gone was that I had a sudden vision of Blake turning up at my front door at any moment. The more I thought about it the more convinced I became that it would happen – the only explanation for him not replying to me was that he wanted to speak to me in person and try and wangle his way into my apartment and bed. It unrolled in my head like a horror film; him at the front door in his pink shirt and ragged jeans, Doris's incredulous face whilst realisation gradually dawned and then my total humiliation when she realised that I was one of the saddos she'd been talking about. It was just too much to bear even thinking about.

Bloody Blake. He could ruin everything. And why does Doris have to know him? Does she know every single person in Frogham? Out of all of her very many undesirable friends and acquaintances why do I have to have a secret affair with one of them? I'll have to move to London or somewhere far, far away where Doris doesn't know everyone.

Or I could confide in her, I suppose. She is my friend.

No. I dismiss the idea instantly. It's not that she'd judge me - although she would – I'd be forever classed as a saddo who had sex with a grubby, creepy sofa surfer - it's that I couldn't bear the pity, or the disgust. I've had enough of both to last me several lifetimes.

I could always get a contract out on him, have him killed off; I have the money.

It's okay I'm only joking.

Probably.

Anyway, he never turned up at my door despite my paranoia and my absolute conviction that he would and the reason he hasn't answered my text is most likely that his phone is dead or he's run out of credit. Honestly, I do let my imagination run away with me sometimes.

I changed into a lovely little black dress with chiffon sleeves and a pair of velvet wedges and put on a touch of make- up for my lunch date. Not for Aiden's benefit, obviously, but for Gerald's. And for my own benefit too; it made me feel better about myself, because the *saddo* comment hurt. Doris had left her *Screaming Siren* lipstick on my dressing table so I applied a good few coatings of that too and it did make me look very different; quite dramatic looking. Maybe I'll use it all of the time now, make it my *look*.

As instructed by Aiden, Gerald and I arrive at three thirty prompt and are now waiting at our table in Langans for Aiden to arrive – he's nowhere to be seen and is going to be at least fifteen minutes late despite telling me to be on time. The absolute cheek of the man.

After I texted Gerald he picked me up en-route so I don't have to worry about driving and I'm debating whether to have a glass of wine to relieve the tedium of Gerald's *going on* and the anticipation of Aiden's monotone drone. Although, actually when I think about it, Gerald isn't *going on*; he's very quiet and seems quite subdued today.

'Everything okay, darling?' I close the wine menu and place it down on the table; I don't think I'll risk it, with the lack of a decent meal I'll get drunk after one glass and I can't bear the thought of Aiden looking down his long, skinny nose at me. I briefly consider having a proper meal instead of a salad but dismiss that idea immediately because I'm so hungry I'm scared I won't be able to control myself and will stuff the whole plateful into my mouth in one go – the same reason I had to forgo the MacDonald's. I'll make up for it later with a binge. Although I'll have to go to the *One Stop* round the corner now because *Tesco's* will be closed. All Aiden's fault.

Gerald smiles. 'No, I'm fine, darling.'

He's not though, I can tell he's not his usual

jolly, garrulous self but I'm prevented from asking further questions because Aiden chooses that moment to arrive. He approaches the table in his usual silent, stealth like manner and silently pulls the chair out, sits down, picks up the menu and studies it. Doesn't even say hello; honestly, I don't know why I tolerate him.

True, he makes me loads of money but truly, I have so much money now that I don't know what to do with it. I could buy a big house as well as my apartment, an uber expensive car, but really, what's the point? I have considered going on a nice holiday somewhere, once I've applied for a passport because I've never had one, but it wouldn't be much fun on my own would it? I'd look like a sad loser. I have considered asking Doris but I don't know if I could stand two solid weeks of her company.

I've never had a holiday in my life; not one. Mother took me on a day trip to Frogley Bay once but my memory of it was that it was miserable; the sky was black and it threatened to rain the whole day and it wasn't much fun sitting on the beach with our coats on. She wouldn't even buy us an ice cream; said that she couldn't afford it and wasn't made of money and to stop asking. I also must have done something wrong or annoyed her in some way because I distinctly remember Mother locking me in the cellar when we got home for some apparent misdemeanour.

'So.' Aiden interrupts my reminiscing by laying

the menu down on the table. 'The awards last night.'

He speaks as if we're picking up on a conversation we've just been having only minutes ago. I carefully and slowly interlace my fingers together on top of the wine list to stop myself from punching him.

'You conducted yourself in an appropriate manner and I've had several conversations this morning with various entities.'

Is this Spock before me? It could very well be because apart from the lack of pointy ears, the pale skin and emotionless demeanour are exactly the same. I say nothing and Gerald jumps in to fill the void.

'Marvellous pictures in the papers this morning. You looked stunning, darling.'

I smile sweetly at Gerald and ignore Aiden.

'*Natural Health* are going to do a feature on you and the book,' Aiden continues, 'I've supplied them with quotes from you and a copy of your book. It should be in next week's edition provided nothing more newsworthy appears.' He pushes a sheet of paper across the table to me and I pick it up to read it. The page is filled with quotes that Aiden has made up and attributed to me and most of them are the usual eat healthy claptrap but halfway down they change. The quotes start referring to the right and wrong way to lose weight, hinting that gastric bands and other extreme diets are not the way to lose weight but that *The Travis Way* most definitely is.

'I've never said anything against gastric bands or any other diets, I don't think I should be quoted as saying this because I don't want to alienate the opposition.'

Aiden waves a hand dismissively. 'It's time to get off the fence because the article they're doing isn't just about you, it's about someone who's had a gastric band.'

'Who?'

'Who what?'

'Who else is the article about?'

Aiden sniffs and takes a miniscule sip of water.

'His name's Warren something or other, I believe. It's going to be a right way versus wrong way sort of article.'

So Warren's been outed then; I didn't think it would take very long. I don't feel comfortable slagging other dieters off, not least because I'm a liar and haven't lost weight the right way at all and I don't want to tempt fate.

'I'd rather those quotes were taken out, they're not what I think at all.'

Aiden makes a strange snorting noise which I *think* is what passes for laughing.

'Too late, it's already been written.'

'But it's not what I said.'

'Doesn't matter. It's what the readers want to hear which is what counts. This Warren person has made a complete liar of himself and been found out so has to pay the price unfortunately.

He'll have a month or two of bad press and then he can disappear back to whatever God forsaken northern town he came from and never be heard of again. Most likely to eat himself to death.'

I don't think I've ever seen Aiden's robotic features so animated and it suddenly hits me why he speaks to me as if I'm an idiot and of no importance at all. It's because I used to be fat; simple as that. In his book fat equals stupid and insignificant.

'And the *Bold Women* producer has been on to me and wants you on the show. Probably at the end of next week.'

I think back to Jackie and Denise and wonder if they know I've been invited onto their show or if the producer has yet to tell them. Although I'm doubtless flattering myself that they'll even know who I am.

'Am I allowed to speak for myself on there or have you written me a script?' I ask Aiden sarcastically.

'Just stick to the usual, although you can keep that sheet of paper and practice what I've written because gastric band Warren will be appearing too.'

'Why? Why would he agree to go on national television to be humiliated by a group of women?'

'He's thick, obviously, probably under some delusion that he's going to be given a chance to give his side of the story,' Aiden says, making that strange snorting laugh again as he pushes his black rimmed glasses further up his skinny nose.

God I hate him.

'Shall we order? Gerald interrupts as a waiter appears silently at the table.

'Watercress salad, please,' I say to the waiter before turning to Aiden and saying brightly, 'Well, let's just hope Warren doesn't shit all over the *Bold Women's* sofa this time.'

Aiden's Adam's apple bobs and I smile nastily at him. 'Are you having today's special, Aiden? It's goulash, I believe.'

CHAPTER SEVEN

I have a quick shower in the guest bathroom and wash and dry my hair to make sure that I look my very best for breakfast – although I have absolutely no food in the house so we'll have to go out and get something.

Or we could go back to bed.

Why am I using the guest bathroom? Because Gerald is in the en-suite and has been for ages, sloshing around, and singing, too. He has quite a nice voice actually, a deep baritone, no doubt he had singing lessons at his private school.

I can't help remembering that Blake used to be in and out of the bathroom in five minutes - if he didn't oversleep and have to dash off to work without showering, which he did most of the time when I come to think about it. I have my suspicions that he never actually got *into* the shower and just ran the water for effect. Maybe he has an aversion to water; you know, like someone with rabies.

Anyway, Gerald. When he dropped me off after we'd finished our meeting with Aiden I invited him in for a coffee – I don't normally do this because usually I've had enough of him and his *going on* by then and I'm keen to get in and be on my own so that I can have something to eat. And I did want to have something to eat because the pathetic watercress salad didn't cut it and I'd barely eaten for days but I *was* a bit worried about Gerald. So although I'd been planning on popping round to the *One Stop* to stock up I was prepared to delay that because Gerald was very quiet throughout the meal and I thought I should find out what was wrong with him. I needed to make sure that it wasn't something that I'd done to upset him without realising.

The fact that he stayed the night is all a bit of a shock, really. And the thing is, because I always think everything is about me, by the time we'd left the *The Langan* and got into the car I'd pretty much concluded that because he's such a nice person he'd decided to do the decent thing and tell me formally that he was withdrawing his proposal of marriage and that the reason he was quiet was because he didn't know how to tell me.

He was silent all the way home in the car and this convinced me even more, so when he pulled up outside I asked if he wanted to come in so we could get it over and done with. He readily agreed and I mentally prepared myself for the worst, although really it was no surprise at all because I'd pretty much worked it out for myself but it's never nice to have these things confirmed.

Typical of Gerald to formally tell me, I thought, as I put the key in the door, anyone else would just hope that I'd got the hint, which I had, and spare themselves the grief. But that's not Gerald's style, because he's honourable.

We came in and I wondered if I even had any milk to put in the coffee and then I thought, *who cares?* Do your worst, Gerald, and get it over with and leave and then it'll just be me and the ghost of Mother for the rest of my life. And occasionally Doris. I'll have my binging and starving to keep me company and I'll probably get some terrible disease because I've abused my body for so long and it'll all serve me right because it's what I deserve.

But no, I'd got it entirely wrong.

The reason he'd been so quiet is that his mother has been ill and she's been having lots of tests to find out what's wrong with her and Gerald and his father had been mentally preparing themselves for the very worst news. I affected a sympathetic expression and tried to feel sorry for him as he was telling me but I wasn't really feeling it. The thing is, I've never even seen a picture of his parents so every time I tried to conjure up an image of them all I could see was a male and female version of Mother. Also, Gerald's never mentioned them before – or he might have done and I wasn't listening - so I'd sort of assumed that they were either dead or that he never saw them and didn't really care about them and that he felt the same way about them that I'd felt about Mother. But that was wrong too because it seems that they're a very close family and always have been and Gerald is an only child, like me, only his parents wanted him and doted on him and think the absolute world of him.

Anyway, I digress. To Gerald and his father's utmost surprise all of the tests came back negative and Gerald's Mother is going to be fine just as soon as she's had her gall bladder removed, which isn't very pleasant but she's not going to die so they had all of that worry for nothing. None of which explained Gerald's long face or why he'd been so quiet until he dropped the bombshell.

He told me that he'd tried to be patient in waiting for my answer as to whether I'd marry him or not but recent events had made him think that life is too short to hang around so he wanted an answer – would I marry him or not?

Incredibly, he actually still wanted to marry me.

Well, what could I say? Yes, of course, and we didn't bother with coffee but opened a bottle of champagne that I just happened to have in my new kitchen wine rack and then we tumbled into bed as befitting our new status as husband and wife to be.

I have to be honest (for once) and say that Gerald was pretty marvellous and didn't make me feel like a novice at all (obviously all of that practice with Blake paid off) and he didn't *go on* at all and it was genuinely wonderful and exactly how having sex - or *making love*, as Gerald calls it, isn't he sweet? - should be.

And I didn't have to mouth breath once.

Sounds like I'm in love, doesn't it?

Of course I'm not, because I don't know what love is but I can't deny that it was all very nice and Gerald is absolutely gorgeous - not to mention clean.

So now I'm just waiting for him to get out of the shower so we can go out for a nice breakfast somewhere to talk about the rest of our lives together – and to talk about our wedding, of course. We haven't talked rings yet but I'm expecting a nice, big, expensive, sparkling rock that I can show off to everyone because Gerald's extremely generous.

He got on the phone to his snooty secretary, Eunice, first thing this morning and told her to push all of today's appointments back to this afternoon because he has an important and urgent matter to deal with this morning. Honestly, I feel all warm and glowing and I don't think it's just from the too hot shower.

I'm just wondering if maybe there is enough milk to make us both a cup of coffee when the doorbell rings; rather persistently as if someone has their finger welded to the buzzer. I expect it's another Amazon parcel for next door; they seem to have deliveries every day but are never around to receive them. The delivery drivers seem to think that it's my job to take in their parcels for them when they're not here and have taken to leaving next doors parcels on *my* doorstep. I do have my suspicions as to whether they're running a business from their apartment. I was thinking about having a word with them to say that I'll refuse future deliveries but as I'm feeling so happy I'll let it go this time.

I pull the front door open with a pleasant expression that quickly turns to horror as the open doorway reveals Blake standing on my doormat. In the split second that it takes my brain to acknowledge his cheap, shiny suit and scuffed shoes I wonder how I could have so easily forgotten about him when I was terrified yesterday that he'd turn up when Doris was here. I've had other much nicer things on my mind obviously but yesterday would have been preferable to today without a doubt, at a push I could have sworn Doris to secrecy, but if Gerald were to see him? Good God, it doesn't bear thinking about.

'Hey, doll, how's it going?' He says through the grey chewing gum clacking around his mouth, which is not an attractive sight at all. What on earth did I ever see in him?

I quickly step outside into the corridor and pull the door nearly closed behind me to prevent Gerald from hearing him.

'What do you want?' I hiss quietly.

'You an' me have things to discuss.'

'No we don't.' I grab hold of his arm and attempt to push him away from the door. 'Now get lost.'

'Don't think so, doll.' He stands rigid and I realise that this isn't going to be so easy.

'Go.' I glare at him.

'What's up? Got someone in there? Got a new boyfriend have you?'

I break out into a sweat at the thought of my soon to be fiancé innocently opening the front door to be greeted by Blake.

'Maybe I could give him a few tips.' He grins. 'You know, tell him what you like.'

I hold his arm tightly and drag and push him along the corridor and down the fire escape stairs to the next floor and push him into the alcove by the cleaners room, all the while aware of his grinning face churning gum around his mouth like a washing machine.

'What do you want? Spit it out and then go.'

'Ooh, you are fired up. I like it when you're all feisty.' He leans back against the wall and folds his arms and looks me up and down. 'I ain't in no hurry, I got all day.'

I glare at him.

'You're looking good, doll.'

'Just tell me what you want.' I demand.

'Like I said in my text, I'm a bit hard up at the mo – thought you could borrow me some money.'

'Lend.'

'What?'

'You want me to lend you some money.'

'Yeah, that's what I said.'

This is pretty much what I was expecting and I think about it for a moment. There's no doubt in my mind that it won't be a loan because he has absolutely no intention or any way of ever paying it back.

'What makes you think I'd lend you money?'

'Well, you're doing really well, ain't you? You've wrote a book and you're in all the papers and on the telly as well. You must be rolling in it.'

'I'm not rolling in it, any money I make has to be reinvested back into the business,' I lie.

He shrugs.

'Tell me why should I lend you my hard earned money?'

'For old time's sake? Weren't that long ago that we were close.'

I put a thoughtful expression on my face as if I'm thinking about it although I've already decided I'm going to have to give him something to get rid of him.

'How much?' I ask.

'Ten grand would see me right.'

'What!' I laugh loudly and then stop myself in case the sound carries up the stairs. 'You must be joking, there's no way I can afford to lend you that, I'm not making *that* much money.' I could easily give him that much but I won't; I think he's started high because he knows I'm going to refuse the first amount. He's an estate agent after all so he's using the same tactic as bidding on a house.

He stares at me without speaking, waiting for me to make him an offer.

'I'll give you a thousand.'

'Okay,' He says ungratefully but his eyes light up, betraying his words.

'But there are conditions,' I go on.

'Okay.'

'Firstly, you *never* come to my home again.'

'Cool.' He waves his hand.

'Secondly, you tell no one – and I mean no one, that we ever knew each other except in a professional capacity when I bought my apartment.'

'Whatever.'

'No. Not whatever. You promise or I'm not lending you anything.'

'I promise, doll, no worries.'

'Okay. I'll text you when I have the money. It probably won't be until the end of the week.'

He looks momentarily disappointed and then nods.

'Cool. Shall I come round Friday and get it?'

'No! Have you forgotten the first condition already? You're *never* to come here again.'

'I won't, calm down, just jesting, doll, just jesting.'

I narrow my eyes at him.

'I promise.'

'Okay. I'll text you when I've got the money and we can meet up somewhere, I'll let you know where.'

'Cool.'

I stare at him.

'What?'

'You need to go now.'

He sniggers and winks and unfolds his arms as he slowly straightens up from leaning on the wall. He brushes by me as he passes and saunters off down the stairs.

'See you Friday, doll,' he calls over his shoulder.

I don't answer but stand looking down over the stairwell railings and watch as he lets himself out of the fire door on the ground floor.

I don't like the thought of giving him money – he calls it a loan but we both know he'll never pay it back. It feels like blackmail. What if he comes back for more? I'll have to get practising with the lying because there's no way I'm going to let him spoil my new life by having some sort of hold over me.

Satisfied that he's gone I go back up the stairs and let myself into the flat, thanking my lucky stars that I left the door slightly open; Gerald need never even know that I've been out.

'Darling! Where have you been?' Gerald, looking box fresh from the shower and as gorgeous as ever, is staring right at me with a perplexed expression on his face as I open the front door.

'Oh! You made me jump! Erm...just popped out to get some milk.'

'So where is it?'

'What?'

'The milk?'

'Silly me - forgot my purse!' I lie. 'I got all the way to the shop on the corner and realised that I didn't have it.'

'Oh, I thought I heard the doorbell.' Gerald frowns slightly.

'No, just me popping out, I should have shut the door really and not left it ajar.'

Gerald's frown deepens. 'I'm here to look after you today, darling, but you shouldn't leave the door open when you're on your own, you never know who could push their way in here.'

I step forward and wrap my arms around his waist and cuddle into him.

'You're completely right, darling, I promise I won't do it again.'

He gently pulls me to him, wraps his arms around me and kisses the top of my head.

'You're too trusting darling.'

Aren't I just?

* * *

We had such a lovely morning; we went to a lovely little café around the corner from Gerald's office for breakfast and toasted our engagement with a glass of fresh orange juice to wash down our *Eggs Benedict*, which were absolutely delicious. Although I'd have eaten a mouldy kebab I was so hungry because all I've eaten since Thursday is two tiny salads – but I did manage to control myself and eat it in a ladylike manner.

I was hoping that we might have fitted in a bit of engagement ring shopping afterwards but Gerald has very definite ideas on that – he wants to use the family jeweller in London as he wants something special and unique and not some tat from Frogham (my words not his). His words were that he didn't think that the jewellers in Frogham would have exactly what he was looking for; honestly, he's such a gentleman.

But before we get the ring he wants us to visit his parents so they can meet me and we can tell them about the engagement as well.

I felt slightly uneasy when he said that; he doesn't want us to tell anyone else about our engagement until we've told them because they should know first. He thinks next weekend would be a good time to visit them; they've retired to a little cottage in Devon and he says that we can treat the visit as a mini holiday.

I can't say I'm looking forward to it. Gerald's a successful solicitor from a good family and I'm an ex-cleaner who was nearly charged with attempted murder; I hardly think I'm going to be welcomed with open arms. But there's no way of getting out of it and I'm keeping my fingers crossed that they haven't seen the *fat me* pictures everywhere, which hopefully they haven't as they'll be far too posh to read the tabloids.

It's just one weekend, I keep telling myself, I can

stand two days of people looking down their nose at me and disliking me because if I can put up with Mother for twenty-eight years I can do pretty much anything.

Gerald says they're going to love me but he would say that, wouldn't he? Gerald sees the good in everyone because let's face it, I've fooled him and what bit of good there might have been in me to start with has been well and truly knocked out of me by Mother. I asked him what I should call his parents – Mr and Mrs Thompson? I can hardly call them Mum and Dad, can I? And when he told me what their names are it just confirmed that they're going to hate me.

Bunty and Jeremy.

I'm not one to prejudge, as you know, but as soon as he told me their names a vision of them popped into my head. Terribly, terribly posh, Bunty will be wafer thin with a cut glass accent and wear orange lipstick whilst Jeremy will ride to hounds and carry a shotgun around at all times.

Honestly, it's enough to make me call the whole thing off.

And then I started thinking about the wedding; apparently Gerald has a huge extended family spread far and wide and I know he has lots of friends and who do I have?

Doris.

She's my only friend so will have to be my bridesmaid but can she keep the accent up for a whole day? Can I trust her not to start effing and jeffing everywhere and getting absolutely rat arsed and show herself, and me, up?

It's enough to drive me straight to the biscuit tin, if I had one. In an attempt to stop myself from a full on massive binge I've decided to take my mind off things by occupying myself with getting rid of the tea chest in the spare room.

The one my father left me. Or rather, the one he left the care home.

I'm going to empty it out and take it all to the tip; it's been there for far too long and I need to man up and get rid of it before I start my new life with Gerald.

After Gerald had dropped me home and zoomed off to work to do lawyerly things, I decided that I'd shilly-shallied long enough and it was time to take the bull by the horns and get on with it.

Armed with a roll of bin liners I march decisively upstairs, determined to consign the mouldy clutter that was my father's legacy to the same place as Mother's lifetime of tat.

Well, almost the same place – I no longer have a garden to have a huge bonfire in so the dustbin will have to suffice.

Time to move on.

Once in the spare room I stand and stare at the tea chest for a while; the throw draped over it is a cheap purple one from Primark that I bought on a whim many years ago when I had ideas of tarting up my old bedroom. I think it's the only thing, aside from the tea chest, that's remains from my old life and that's going to be the first thing to go. I drag it off the tea chest but it catches on a nail and I tug it smartly and it rips before coming away and I give it a good yank and it makes a satisfying ripping sound. Once released I swiftly roll it up into a bundle and stuff it into the bin bag.

I stand over the tea chest and peer inside; grubby looking books and a jumble of what looks like spectacle cases and assorted bric-a-brac lie on the top and I realise that I need one more thing before I start this distasteful job. I leave the bedroom and return to the kitchen – not to stuff my face with fortifying binge food because I haven't got any but to get some rubber gloves – there's no way I'm touching any of that tat without them. Fortunately, I have several brand new pairs under the sink although I've never used any of them; no doubt when I was looking for things to buy they looked like a good idea at the time.

I return to the bedroom with my hands suitably sheathed in pink latex and start removing items from the chest. Many, many spectacle cases with very similar tortoiseshell spectacles inside each one of them. How many pairs of glasses does one person need and why keep them all? I have no idea and I hold one pair open in front of my eyes to look through them and deduce that my late father was practically blind. I consign them all to the bin bag along with the mouldy looking books that have dust lodged into the page edges.

My heart skips a beat when I pull out an ancient

picture frame; a brown age spotted picture of my late father and a dark haired horsey looking woman on their wedding day, this must be the wife that Mother hated so much. She's no beauty but she looks very happy; as does my father and I study the black and white photograph to see if I resemble him at all. I decide that I don't and consign the frame complete with photograph into the bin bag along with bundles of old hospital appointments and repeat prescriptions. Several moth-eaten jumpers, still wrapped Christmas presents of *Old Spice* and assorted toiletries from *all the staff*, a heavy tweed dressing gown and a pair of slippers with a hole in one sole are all that is left of my father. I wonder what happened to the rest of his clothes? Perhaps they were recycled for the other residents or maybe everyone's wardrobe was interchangeable.

If I cared at all I'd feel sad; it's not much to show for a life lived and it's not as if there's anyone left to grieve for him. If he hadn't been so gutless he'd have had a daughter who would have missed him. I'm pleased now that I won't suffer the same fate as Mother and my father now – Gerald will grieve for me at least.

I fill three bags and tie the tops of them into knots in readiness for putting in the car although I'm not sure how I'll fit a tea chest in my MX5 – I may have to ask Gerald to take that for me which is a shame because now I've emptied it I want rid of it.

The doorbell shrills sharply and I catch my breath; surely not Blake again? No, I'm being ridiculous, he won't want to jeopardise the thousand pounds I'm going to give him on Friday. I drag the bin bags with me and leave them in the hallway before opening the front door. There's no one there but there are three large boxes from Amazon on my doormat; next doors deliveries again. I'm about to shove them along the corridor to next door when I have a better idea and close the front door.

I go back into the bedroom and drag the empty tea chest out into the hall and as I drag it along I realise that I haven't emptied it completely because there's something wrapped in newspaper rolling around in the bottom of it. That's annoying; I'll have to untie a knot on a bin bag that I tied super tight, to chuck it in there. I take out the newspaper wrapped bundle and place it on the floor so I can deal with it afterwards. I drag the tea chest along to the front door, open the door and pick up next door's Amazon parcels from my door mat and place them inside the tea chest. I stand back and admire my handiwork; almost made to measure because they practically fill it. I drag the tea chest over the threshold and along the corridor to the apartment next door and place it neatly on their doormat.

There. That'll learn 'em, as Doris would say.

I go back into my apartment and mindful of Gerald's warning about leaving doors open, I close the door while I get some shoes on to take the bags to the tip; I can wedge one bag in the boot and the other two will fit on the passenger seat. I pick the newspaper wrapped parcel up from the floor and heft it in my hand; it's as heavy as a house brick and the size of a large jam jar - before I can change my mind and start imagining a set of false teeth or a jar of something horrible I quickly unwrap it and hold it in my gloved hands.

I turn it around slowly and acknowledge that it's probably one of ugliest ornaments that I've ever seen and that's saying something because Mother had some horrors. A very odd looking, beige and grey pottery bird with a massive hooked beak and huge claw type hands. The head lifts off completely so it must be meant for storing something although God knows what because who'd want to eat a biscuit out of something as hideous as that? It has horrible hooded eyes that seem to be looking right at me and the beak is somehow sneering. I'm about to attempt to untie a bin bag and toss it in when something stops me.

Those eyes, that expression, where have I seen them before?

I can't remember but for some unknown reason I decide to keep it, a memento if you like, of my late father.

And it sort of looks like Mother.

CHAPTER EIGHT

We're on our way to Devon, Gerald and I, to see his parents so that we can tell them about our engagement before we make it public. I did suggest that he just rang them and told them to save us going all of that way but Gerald gave me such a strange look that I had to pretend I was joking. I have to keep reminding myself that his parents aren't like Mother; that most parents aren't like Mother.

I can't say I'm looking forward to meeting them; I'm viewing it as something that has to be got out of the way before we can go ring shopping and announce our engagement officially. Gerald doesn't seem to see his parents on a regular basis even though he's told me that they're close, he says he gets down to Devon as often as possible but it's difficult with his business. I'm not really sure what his definition of *close* is as he was packed off to boarding school when he was seven years old so he can't have seen that much of them when he was growing up, can he?

I wish I'd been packed off to boarding school when I was seven; although even seven years old might have been too late to grow up untouched by the madness of mother. Maybe if I'd been sent away at birth I'd have escaped unscathed.

Unless it's hereditary, of course.

With a bit of luck visiting them won't be something that we have to do very often; I could cope with once or twice a year.

We had intended driving down first thing this morning but Gerald had an emergency meeting with one of his clients so it was past two o'clock by the time we left Frogham. I shouldn't think that there are many solicitors who would disrupt their Saturday morning for an urgent meeting with a client; this is why Gerald's so successful – he goes the extra mile.

I'm actually pleased about the late departure and think that it's a good thing because it's less time for me to let myself down in front of Bunty and Jeremy and prove to them that I'm not the right girl for their son.

The journey seems to be taking forever and although I'm in no rush to arrive the narrow, twisting, Devon lanes are starting to make me feel a bit sick. I press the button to open the window to let some fresh air into the car, put my head back against the headrest and close my eyes.

'You okay, darling?' Gerald asks with concern in his voice.

'Fine. Just a little car sick, that's all.'

'I didn't realise that you don't travel well.'

Nor did I, not ever having been anywhere further than London. I would have taken some travel sickness pills if I'd known. I'm fine on my regular trips to London but that journey is less than an hour - and it's motorway all the way and not these awful B roads. It's just my luck and a bad omen I'm sure; I'll probably get out of the car and throw up all over Bunty's brogues.

I take some deep breaths of the fresh air coming through the window and start to feel a bit better. Gerald gets the hint and slows down a bit too, which helps because he drives very fast which doesn't go well with winding lanes; I feel as if I've been having a ride on a very fast roller coaster. He also stops *going on*, which was starting to get rather wearing, constant shop talk about some important case he's preparing which I'd tried to zone out but being trapped in a confined space with him was proving difficult. I felt that I had to make appropriate comments and at least appear to be listening but it's quite exhausting after a while. I don't know how he can expend so much energy talking so much – he must have a lot of stamina and how does he even think of things to talk about? Maybe it's me but I can convey all I need to in a few sentences, I don't need to relate every second of what happened in my day from the moment I opened my eyes in the morning. Although I'm probably being unfair because it's the only fault that Gerald has that I've discovered so far and I've known him for quite a long time now so he must be a genuinely *good* person – or an accomplished liar, like me.

I don't think he is a liar though, because it takes one to know one.

In the past two weeks since we've been unofficially engaged, Gerald and I have spent a lot of our evenings together when I haven't been doing book promotions and he hasn't been working. Fortunately, last night he had a business dinner with a client which suited me just fine as I don't want to get too sick of him or for him to get tired of me. You can have too much of a good thing and also there's no chance of me bingeing when he's around. I know I can binge in the daytime but it's not the same; for some reason I prefer to evening binge; maybe it's because I can just go to bed and sleep it all off afterwards.

Although as it turned out I haven't binged as much as I thought I would because I haven't been *that* hungry – which is a good thing because I really need to get out of the habit because I won't be able to do it when we're married and living together. I think maybe my stomach has shrunk with all of the starving that I do. And I do need to take my foot off the pedal, weight wise, once we're hitched; maybe I can eat normally then and put a bit of weight on and be more, well, normal. I'll have to have a good think about it but I definitely think it's the way to go.

Blake has been dealt with and is now in the past – I paid him the thousand pounds that I promised and have impressed on him that he's never to contact me again – either by text or in person and I've heard nothing from him since and that was over a week ago. I didn't want him coming to my apartment to get the money and I didn't want to go to his place – if he even has one, which I have my doubts about. After a lot of brain racking I told him to meet me at the payment station on the third floor of the multi storey car park in town. I told him that if there was anyone else using the machine he had to wait until they'd gone before approaching me. Luckily, there was no one about and as soon as I saw him waiting I marched up to him and shoved the envelope of cash into his hand and then marched away.

I felt a bit like a spy in an old film and Blake thought it was over the top, *I can pick it up from urs doll,* he'd texted even though I'd told him never to come to my apartment again. No, I don't want him anywhere near my apartment and I don't want to take the risk of being seen in public with him either. I even checked before I agreed to meet him that there weren't any security cameras in the car park because you never know who's watching and I certainly didn't want a digital record of our meeting floating around somewhere. I'm happy now that he's out of my life forever and as far as I'm concerned a thousand pounds was a very small price to pay.

'We're here darling.'

I drag my thoughts back to the here and now and my heart sinks at the thought of the weekend ahead but I compose my features into a pleasant smile and open my eyes. Although I've dreaded arriving I'll be glad to get out of the car and get some proper fresh air and stretch my legs.

I look through the window and stare open mouthed as we drive past the house. 'I thought you said your parents lived in a little cottage?' I can't keep the shock from my voice because I can't believe what I'm actually seeing. The house is *huge*; more country pile than country cottage. The road that we're driving on is a driveway that sweeps grandly down to the front of a white washed stone house. We continue past the house and pull to a stop in front of a barn type building with two sets of double doors, which I guess is garages. Gerald executes a neat three-point turn and reverses into the space in front of one of them and kills the engine. I sit and gawp at the house; three storeys high with tall windows, the front door is twice the height and width of my own front door and I count ten windows on the top floor alone.

Gerald turns and looks at me in puzzlement.

'It *is* tiny compared to their old place.'

'My God,' I shriek. 'What did they live in before, a castle?'

For once Gerald doesn't speak but looks slightly uncomfortable and the truth dawns on me.

'They really *did* live in a castle?'

'Well, yes, I suppose you could call it that but it was only a very small one.' He opens the car door and swings his legs out. 'Come on, let's get inside and get a drink, get rid of your car sickness.'

I pull myself out of the car and stretch and as I gaze at the house I half expect to see a row of servants lined up waiting to curtsey as they greet us.

I breathe in fresh air and stretch and roll my neck as Gerald gets our bags out of the boot.

I can do this.

We head towards the house and I keep reminding myself that it's just one weekend and it'll soon be over.

'You'll be telling me they're royalty next.' I joke, as we crunch across the gravel towards the house.

Gerald laughs and takes hold of my hand. 'They're just ordinary, darling.'

I smile up at him in my best fiancé way.

'Besides,' he says, as we reach the house, 'Daddy hardly ever uses his title anyway.'

I thought I knew what Bunty and Jeremy would be like – mega posh (which they are, because Jeremy is a Baron, whatever that is, I'll be asking Mr Google later). When Bunty opened the door, at first I thought she was one of the servants, perhaps the cleaner, because she was nothing like I was expecting. The first shock, the BIGGEST shock was the size of her.

She is immense.

Bigger than I was, much bigger, with the most enormous bust that I've ever seen. She doesn't wear orange lipstick or wear a tweed suit or brogues but she does look very like Gerald; a female, obese version of him, obviously. She's what you'd call a handsome woman; thick black hair, flecked with grey, coiled neatly into a fat bun and a perfectly made up face. She seemed to be wearing a floor length dress made from some sort of blackout material and I could see fuchsia coloured fluffy mules peeking out from below the hem.

'Darlings! At last!' She screamed as she stretched two humungous arms out and grabbed Gerald and crushed him to her mammoth chest and wrapped her arms around him. I stood there gawping like an idiot and desperately tried to think of something to say and the hug lasted so long I wondered if she might suffocate him in her bosom. Once she'd finished with Gerald she thrust him away - luckily he was still breathing - looked me up and down, muttered *lovely, lovely* and then grabbed me by the shoulders and pulled me to her. I didn't quite know what to do when she did that so stood quite awkwardly with my arms hanging down while she nearly hugged me to death. I'm not used to such shows of affection and I'm not completely sure that I like it.

She held me very tightly and then let me go so suddenly that I nearly fell over. She turned to the open doorway behind her and shrieked *Jeremy* so loudly that I thought it might burst my eardrums.

Gerald stood there with this funny look on his face; soppy, I suppose you'd call it. We all waited for Jeremy to appear and I half expected him to pop out from underneath Bunty's voluminous dress.

'GERALD, M'BOY!'

With the booming voice of a cannon, Jeremy appeared from behind Bunty. Fat, but not as big as Bunty, Jeremy was attired in yellow *Rupert the Bear* type tweed trousers topped off with a grubby green sweater with holes in the sleeves. I was relieved to see that he didn't have a shotgun. He didn't hug Gerald but grabbed his hand between both of his huge paws and proceeded to pump Gerald's hand up and down as if he were cranking an engine. Gerald beamed at him and then turned and introduced me.

Jeremy made no secret of the fact he was looking me up and down and then he put his huge hands on my shoulders and kissed me on both cheeks.

'Lovely to meet you, m'dear, Gerald's told us all about you. We thought you'd never say yes.'

They knew about me. I was utterly shocked. They knew he'd asked me to marry him and I've said yes, so we'd come all of this way to tell them what they already knew. The funny look on Gerald's face when I suggested he ring them was guilt because he already *had* rung them, so he's not an accomplished liar like me which I'd more or less guessed but it's nice to have it confirmed. Gerald is a good person; far too good for me – which I should feel bad about for his sake, but I don't because I'm *not* a good person.

Greetings completed, Bunty and Jeremy herded us through the doorway into the massive hallway of the house and then manoeuvred us in a sheep-dog like way into a huge room full of overstuffed sofas and mammoth pieces of furniture looming over us from the edges of the room.

'Sit down, m'dear, sit down.' Jeremy waved his hand in the air and I sat down gingerly on a ruby red velvet sofa and kept on sinking downwards until I was practically lying down.

'Oops, you've picked the one I usually sit on,' Bunty said as she flopped down onto the candy-striped sofa opposite me, 'I'm afraid I've quite ruined it with all my weight. Jeremy usually has to give me a hand to get out of it.'

I stared at her in amazement; she'd mentioned her weight and didn't seem in the slightest bit ashamed or apologetic about it.

I hauled myself up from the sofa and went over and sat next to her and Gerald sat himself on the other side of her. Jeremy muttered something about making tea and plodded back out through the door into the hallway.

'Now.' Bunty took one of my hands in hers. 'You must tell me all about yourself, my dear, and make sure that you leave nothing out.'

* * *

I didn't have to tell Bunty very much, as it turned out, because Gerald had pretty much told them everything about me; even that I'd cared for my elderly mother and been arrested for attempted murder, although in his version I was a devoted carer who'd selflessly given up her own life to look after Mother.

As it became apparent how much he'd told them about me I realised that I had no idea how smitten with me he really is. Bunty did most of the talking and she asked me lots of questions about my book – she said she'd read it from cover to cover and was very impressed with it. She said that she would have definitely tried the diet when she was younger but she wasn't going to bother now because it was all too much like hard work. She's not at all embarrassed about her size and says she has no intention of ever going on another diet because it's too boring and life's too short.

When Jeremy reappeared, trundling an enormous wooden trolley bearing teapot, cups and saucers and several large cake stands filled with cakes, Bunty insisted that he pick up their wedding photograph from the piano (yes, really they have a grand piano in their lounge or maybe that should that be drawing room) so that I could see that they hadn't always been fat – although Jeremy is nowhere near the size of Bunty. They were very slim when they got married and Bunty was very pretty and Jeremy very handsome so I can see where Gerald gets his good genes from. I said what a lovely picture it was and Jeremy bent down and kissed the top of Bunty's head and said she hadn't changed one bit since the day he married her. Bunty giggled girlishly and then Jeremy lumbered over to the piano to put the picture back. He huffed and puffed back over to us and practically threw himself into the red sofa opposite although unlike me he managed to stay sort of upright.

So today has been so much better than I imagined; I like Bunty and Jeremy, I like them very much. Warm, funny and straight talking, I think Gerald is a very lucky man indeed to have such great parents.

I know that it's just the luck of the draw and I could have done a lot worse and had a serial killer for a mother but I couldn't help feeling a bit jealous. Gerald gets a couple of absolute gems who also happen to be stinking rich, whereas I got Mother, the booby prize. It's probably why Gerald is such a nice man, because he is, even with his *going on*, whereas I'm not a nice person but I am trying and I think maybe I can be a better person now - because I have no reason not to be and with good people around me, who knows?

I think I'm definitely going to stop the binging too because I really don't think Gerald would be that bothered if I put on a few pounds and wasn't a tiny size eight any more. I even managed to eat a couple of cakes without stuffing them in whole whilst we were sitting chatting in the lounge so

I think I could do it. It would be so nice to eat normally and not have to do the starve and binge thing anymore because I'm sure it's not a healthy way to live, quite apart from the food cravings I'm sure it's not doing my body any good. Maybe my periods will come back if I'm a more normal weight although to be honest I can't say I've missed them; they're a bloody nuisance, pardon the pun. But that's not normal is it, not having periods? It just proves that I don't weigh as much as I should.

I do feel that I've definitely turned a corner; I've found a man who adores me and I have a new life to look forward to and I can finally put the past, and Mother, behind me. I'm going to make the effort to make some more friends as well; I don't think it's healthy to only have one friend. Maybe I'll get a hobby or join a club or something; I'm sure there are lots of things that I could do if I looked into it, although it's all very time consuming and tedious because I only want *suitable* friends, if you know what I mean. It'd be much easier if you could, oh I don't know, buy them or something.

I stretch my arms and legs out in the humungous bed in Gerald's bedroom – although he's never actually lived here Bunty and Jeremy have allotted him a bedroom and furnished and decorated it especially for him which is, I think, rather sweet and wonderful of them. The bed is so soft and comfortable and feels so luxurious with the heavy cotton sheets edged with satin. Even lying in the middle with my arms outstretched I can't quite reach the sides. I'm feeling quite smug, which is a feeling that I've never had before. I definitely feel that my life is on track at long last. I wouldn't even mind if we visited Bunty and Jeremy quite often because they're so nice and so easy to get along with and for some reason they seem to like *me*. They kept saying what a lucky man Gerald is and how they're so thrilled to welcome me to the family. They could be liars too but I don't think they are because they're too *nice*. I think I might have to pinch myself to make sure I'm not having a lovely dream.

My phone pings from the bedside table; do I answer it or leave it? It'll be Doris, wanting to know how I've got on meeting *the 'rents* as she calls them. I told her where we were going, but not that we're getting engaged as I don't think Doris could keep a secret although I think she's probably guessed because why else would I go all the way to Devon to meet Gerald's parents? If I told her I don't think she'd blab deliberately it's just that she can't help herself so I'm always selective about what I tell her. I'm tempted to not read the message and leave it until the morning but Gerald is taking such a long time to clean his teeth that I might as well. I roll over on the bed and pick my phone up from the bedside table and look at the screen to see that it's not Doris at all.

It's Blake.

For God's sake, trust him to interrupt my

weekend. I haven't heard from him since I gave him the money and there's only one reason he'd be contacting me – he wants more. Well he's not getting any, he's had all he's getting out of me. I knew this would happen, he seems to be under some illusion that I still have feelings for him and will therefore keep doling out money to him.

Should I just get it over with and tell him now that he's not getting anything else out of me? I think I will; it'll be done and dusted and then and I can block him on WhatsApp straight afterwards so he can't keep sending me whinging texts. I don't need him hanging around like a bad smell spoiling my lovely new life and I definitely don't want him pestering me with badly written text messages all weekend.

I tap the screen to open the message and for a moment I can't make sense of it, it's not a text but a photograph. I squint and hold it closer to study it and my stomach flips when I eventually realise what it is. It's a picture of me lying face down on my bed, the sheets thankfully covering me from the waist down and I look very much as if I'm asleep, which I must have been because I'd never have allowed him to take a picture of me if I was awake. My hair is messy and half hanging over my face but there's no denying that it's me.

But that isn't the worst part.

A grinning Blake, hairy chest proudly on display, is lying next to me and it's very obvious that we've spent the night together. I thought I'd been so careful about him taking pictures of us together but I never thought he'd take one when I was asleep. I shudder when I think what other photographs he might have taken without me knowing.

Ping!

It is a message this time and I open it with a sinking heart.

Hey doll sorry to bother u but I find myself in financial difficulties and need another loan

Blackmail.

I flip my phone to silent and place it face down on the bedside table.

I knew it was too good to last.

What the hell am I going to do?

CHAPTER NINE

Blake blighted the entire weekend; I tried not to think about him but the minute that I started to relax and enjoy myself up he'd pop; his stupid grinning face and that horrible hairy chest taunting me.

Why? Why was I so stupid? What on earth did I ever see in him? There is *nothing* remotely attractive about him and the thought of him in my bed repulses me.

I repulse me.

What was I thinking?

I eventually replied to his message – a brief *what do you want?* - and he waited until this morning to reply; probably so that I'd be more likely to give in and pay him whatever he asks for.

Ten would be great doll same place?

I've no doubt he means ten thousand which I can easily afford but where will it end? He's being very careful with what he's saying in his texts so he's not as stupid as I think he is. What *can* I do?

He has a compromising picture of me and I can't do anything about it so I'll just have to pay him.

Or pay a hit man, ten grand would most likely be enough to get him killed off but I don't think there are too many hit men hanging around Frogham and how would I find one? They're hardly likely to advertise their services in the local newspaper and knowing my luck I'd get caught and end up in prison.

I'm only joking, of course.

Although it would be extremely convenient if he were to get run over by a bus in the near future.

I can't keep on paying him; this has to end.

I need to get it sorted and get rid because I can't be thinking about it all of the time, Gerald and I are going up to London at the weekend to look at rings but the Blake thing is ruining everything so I'm not even looking forward to that. Why is it that the very minute that my life is working out exactly how I want it to, something happens to spoil it? Why did the very person I chose to have an affair with have to be a black mailer who took the opportunity to take a picture of me while I was sleeping so he could use it at a later date? It's not normal behaviour for most people but I had to meet the one person who did it.

Honestly, it's enough to drive me to drink.

Gerald says he doesn't want to announce our engagement until I have the ring on my finger and *then* we can invite our friends out to a celebratory dinner and make the announcement. Although it'll be all of his friends and only Doris from my side; perhaps Gerald's friends will become mine.

As long as that photograph never sees the light of day because we won't be announcing anything if Blake doesn't keep his mouth shut.

And if that wasn't enough to be thinking about I have to prepare myself for tomorrow, too. I'm making an appearance on *Bold Women* and I need to make sure that I come across well because Denise and Jackie are known to be brutal if they don't like you. I was supposed to be on there a couple of weeks ago but a well-known soap star got caught drink-driving so they cleared the decks of all scheduled interviews. This was so they could wheel people on who'd had dealings with the disgraced soap star and were prepared to slag them off royally whilst pretending to be concerned for their mental health. It was vicious – I usually only watch it by accident but in view of my upcoming appearance I thought I'd better get the low down on it and see exactly what I'd let myself in for so I watched all of the current series on *catch up*.

I'm going to have to be so careful that I say all of the right things in all the right places so Denise and Jackie don't take a dislike to me. I might not be very nice but those two are on another level; bitchy, mock concerned, bigoted and spiteful in the extreme. According to Aiden, Warren from Doncaster is going to be the fall guy so they've already got it in for him but I can't take anything for granted. They could suddenly change their minds and turn on me if I say something they don't like. I've seen them rip into people for no apparent reason that I can fathom and it isn't pretty.

I need to be condemning about Warren's gastric band, but I have to do it so I don't look nasty; I have to be damning but in a nice way. He must be mad to have agreed to go on the show and if I was him I definitely wouldn't; I'd be lying low and waiting for it all to blow over.

I'm not looking forward to the show at all and unthinkingly I again reach for my phone to text Blake.

What do I say?

I need to get the photograph off him and any more that he might have taken. I'm guessing they're only on his phone because he's told me himself that he's *computer illiterate* – a pun which he thought was very clever and hilarious - even though he managed to hold down a job in an estate agents so I don't think he'll have them saved anywhere else. I hope. I'll make him delete them in front of me and hope for the best. I might as well just get it over with so I quickly type:

I should have the money by Friday. Will message you in the morning to arrange to meet.

I hit *send* before I can change my mind and feel marginally better; I'm only stalling him but it'll give me more time to think and plan what to do. There *must* be something I can do; I just haven't thought of it yet.

I see from the screen that Blake is *typing* so he must have been constantly looking at his phone and waiting for me to reply. Sure enough my phone pings within seconds.

Ok doll don't let me down

There's a threat there, I can feel it, but at least I've bought myself some breathing space. I need to find out a few facts, the main one being can someone take a photograph of you in a compromising position without your knowledge or permission and show it to other people? I don't think they can, I'm pretty sure that I've heard there's a law against it. I quickly open the browser on my phone and Google it and discover that it *is* illegal. *Revenge porn* is against the law and can result in a prison sentence, so in theory Blake could be arrested and charged.

Which is all very well but I don't think it'll stop him; he'll shoot first and ask questions later. Even if he *was* arrested and charged once the picture's out there it's a bit late and a bit pointless, it'd be all over the internet in a flash. Blackmail is also illegal but realistically once Gerald has seen that photograph he's going to be asking me some very searching questions. I don't think I'll be able to lie my way out of it and I can see our engagement being called off in a flash. He won't understand why I had sex with Blake and not him and I don't think the *I was practising* line is going to cut it. How do I explain Blake away when I've been acting like the virgin Mary, telling Gerald that I'm not ready?

I can visualise the disgust on Gerald's face and my bright new future will rapidly disappear down the toilet and that's without it being splashed all over Facebook.

Which I wouldn't even know about until it was too late because I'm not *on* Facebook.

Oh my God what if it's on there already?

No. It can't be; because Doris practically lives on Facebook and knows absolutely everyone so she'd have seen it and told me. Besides, Blake wouldn't be so stupid as to go public because then there'd be no need for me to pay him.

And what if there are more photographs that are even worse? A vision of Blake arranging my naked, slumbering body into an array of poses makes me gag and I rush to the bathroom and throw up, which is mostly bile because I've hardly eaten a thing.

I hang over the toilet bowl wondering what I'm going to do; I can't go on like this, it's ridiculous. I've felt sick all weekend and I couldn't even face binging when I got home from Gerald's parent's last night. I simply couldn't face the thought of eating anything and it's all Blake's fault.

I don't think I've ever not felt like eating, *ever*. Perhaps I could market it as the *worry diet*; make some really stupid blunder in your life that's basically going to ruin it forever and Bob's your uncle; you can't bear to eat.

I could kill Blake.

* * *

Warren and I are waiting in the green room; we'll be called to go through to the studio as soon as the presenters are in place on *Bold Women*. I spent most of yesterday veering between absolute conviction that Blake is going to ruin my life interspersed with moments of telling myself not to be so stupid and dramatic and to *get a fucking grip*, as Doris would say. If it wasn't for the fact that I don't trust anyone I'd confide in Doris because I feel as if my head's going to explode with it all whirling around. I try to imagine what her advice would be if I told her but find that I can't get past the look of incredulity and pity on her face when I confess to having had an affair with Blake.

No. I'll just have to deal with it alone as I've done with everything else in my life. I can't remember feeling as bad as this for a long time. I feel worse than I did during the ten years of looking after Mother because I had no hope then and nothing to lose. I thought I'd never have a life and I'd resigned myself to being miserable forever so it couldn't really get any worse no matter what I did. Now I have so much to lose.

When I woke up this morning I told myself that I'm not having another day like yesterday; I forced myself to eat some toast even though I didn't want anything and every time Blake's grinning face popped into my head I pinched the skin on the back of my hand to stop myself going into a downward spiral. I don't know what it's supposed to do but I read about it in a mental health article and it can't hurt, well apart from the actual pinch, can it? I suppose the pinch reminds me not to think of him and make a conscious effort to think about something else. I need to think of a way to get Blake out of my life and stop him ruining it – I managed to turn my life around even though Mother had ruled me for years so getting rid of Blake should be easy. Blake is no match for Mother. I pinch the back of my hand; I can't think about it today, I'll think about it tomorrow, defer the worrying.

I concentrate on the now, and I go over in my head the answers to the questions that I pretty much know that Denise and Jackie are going to ask me. I sneak a sideways look at Warren; he's slumped on the sofa opposite me staring gloomily into space. He doesn't look as if he's put any weight on and he's not touched any of the croissants and coffee on offer. I think he's actually *lost* weight; maybe he's on the worry diet too and he can't bear to eat either. He's come on the show to try and publicly explain why he lied about cycling all of those miles to lose weight and if he's hoping to get the public's forgiveness he's in for a horrible shock. Has he ever watched the show? I think the very fact that he's here is proof that he's never seen one single episode.

I've tried to start a conversation with him but he gave one word answers so I guess he's not in the mood for chit chat. Part of me wanted to tell him to leave while he still could because I'm positive he has no idea what he's letting himself in for. Maybe it's better that I don't get into a conversation with him as I'm going to be aiding and abetting Denise and Jackie in humiliating and belittling him so I don't want to get friendly with him and put myself off from slagging him off. In a nice way, of course.

I can't help feeling sorry for him though – probably because I've lied too so he's no different from me. What will I do if I'm found out? How would I explain that *The Travis Way* is a load of rubbish and that really I starved myself? It's no good; I can't imagine it because there's no way anyone could possibly find out because I'm the only one who knows. But Warren's hardly committed a crime has he? He's lied about how he lost weight but I can't see that it matters because having a gastric band operation doesn't seem any easier than sticking to a diet; it plainly doesn't take away the craving for food otherwise he wouldn't be mashing up doughnuts so he could drink them. Major surgery versus sticking to a diet – I know which I'd go for although obviously my personal preference is binging and starving.

A perky blonde with a ponytail pops her head around the door and interrupts my thoughts.

'You're on!' she trills. 'Follow me please.'

Warren and I have barely got out of our seats

before she disappears back through the doorway and we have to trot to keep up with her as we weave our way through long narrow corridors that seem to stretch for miles. We follow her bobbing ponytail for what seems like forever and by the time we eventually reach the studio Warren's face is puce with a shiny film of sweat on it and he's struggling to catch his breath. I wonder if the perky blonde deliberately raced along at speed to try and wrong foot us but immediately dismiss the thought; she's just one of those annoying gym bunnies who do everything super cheerfully and at warp speed.

Perky holds her clipboard up in front of us and we stop and stand at the side of the studio as a make-up artist brushes powder onto Jackie's face. The studio manager waves a hand and Warren and I follow Perky as she bounces across the floor to our allotted seats.

Denise and Jackie sit behind a reception like counter which covers their bottom halves whilst four chairs have been placed in front of them at right angles to the counter, facing them but about six feet away. This is a surprise because when I've watched *Bold Women* on television it appears that the guest seats are right next to Jackie and Denise, oh, the magic of television.

Perky indicates with her clipboard that Warren and I should take our seats. I congratulate myself on my choice of outfit - silky navy trousers and a cream top - because the guest seats are stool like affairs that are difficult to get onto with any degree of elegance and trousers will make sure I don't flash my knickers to the entire studio. Once I've managed to scramble up I realise that they have completely useless low metal backs that finish just above the cheeks of my bottom which means that I can't lean back and will have to perch uncomfortably upright. They also don't have a bar to rest my feet on so my feet dangle uselessly in front of me. I can hear Warren huffing and puffing as he attempts to heave himself onto the stool and when the puffing seems to have abated I risk a glance at him.

He sits rigidly, straight backed and unmoving and looks perched so precariously that if he moves even slightly he'll surely fall off. I know how he feels; thankfully our allotted time slot is short so we won't have to sit like this for very long – the other two empty chairs on the other side of Denise and Jackie must be for the guests due on after us. I wonder if it's deliberate, the uncomfortable seats designed to make us feel vulnerable and awkward. I notice that Jackie and Denise are seated on much more substantial affairs with high, padded backs and they no doubt have rungs to rest their feet on.

'Hi, I'm Tarquin, second studio manager.' A fifteen-year-old wearing glasses with thick black frames and a head of mousy hair coiled into a scraggy bun pops up in front of us.

'A couple of things,' he carries on speaking without waiting for us to acknowledge him,

'Firstly, the camera will be on you from the waist up when you speak so look straight at the camera. Got that? No turning your head or looking at other people otherwise you're just going to look weird.'

Without waiting for an answer, he carries on.

'Secondly, no waffling. Quick, concise answers. If you see me do this.' He makes a throat cutting gesture with his hands. 'You need to shut up.' With that he turns smartly on his stacked heels and prepares to march off but Warren's plaintive voice stops him in his tracks.

'Tarquin?'

'Yes?' Tarquin turns around and glares at Warren, he looks annoyed.

'Do you think the make-up lady could come over and put a bit of powder on me? Maybe take the shine off?'

'No.' He's already turned and marching away. 'Our make-up artists only do the presenters.' He taps smartly across the studio.

That confirms it; the uncomfortable seats and no make-up are deliberate and designed to put you on the back foot so they have the upper hand. I got made up very nicely for my breakfast television appearances and the sofas were comfortable and all of the studio staff tried to put me at ease. I look across at Denise and Jackie; they haven't even acknowledged that Warren and I are here and two more people are being trundled over to sit on the other two seats and they're ignored as well. We're only six feet away, right in front of them and they haven't even looked at us.

The weekly gossip magazines are always featuring Jackie and Denise, their husbands, children and seemingly hundreds of relations from their huge, extended families. Each week there are spreads detailing their heated bust ups, reconciliations, new homes and holidays, cosmetic procedures and cancer scares. It seems as if the public can't get enough of them and their lives.

People are always desperate to get on this show because it has such a massive audience and if Jackie and Denise take a shine to you then you can't go wrong; they'll even mention you in their interviews with the gossip magazines and promote you for all they're worth.

But if they don't like you? Well it'll be publicity but not in a good way. Denise and Jackie are quite volatile and opinionated and seem to be able to get away with saying whatever they like and a lot of people have rued the day that they ever came on the show. Warren must be very naive to think that he can tell his side of the story and receive a fair hearing. He can't ever have watched the show because one of their favourite gambits is to get two people on with opposing views who can start a debate that Denise and Jackie swiftly whip up into a screaming argument, which the public absolutely love. I'm hopeful that Denise and Jackie will favour me because Denise was once a bit of a porker and never tires of telling the audience how losing weight has changed her life – in theory I *should* be okay.

A grey haired man is shouting and I look over to see that Jackie and Denise have pulled themselves upright from their slightly slumped positions and have replaced their pinched mouths and frowns with the pleasant expressions that their viewers love.

'Live in ten!' The grey haired man shouts as he starts a countdown, punctuating each number with an up and down arm movement. My stomach flips and I take a deep breath and slowly exhale. It won't be long and it'll all be over.

'Hello and welcome to Bold Women.' Denise beams at the camera. 'Today we're going to be taking a look at the dieting world and the right and wrong way to go about losing weight.' She turns to Jackie who takes over and I wonder if they count the words they say so that one doesn't get more than the other; I wouldn't be surprised.

'So let's get this party started by introducing our first guests for today, Alison Travis and Warren Strickland.'

From behind the camera Tarquin mimes a big smile with his fingers so I smile and stare at the camera, feeling like an idiot.

'So, Alison, I think I'm right in saying that your diet book, *The Travis Way*, is one of the most successful and fastest selling diet books this year. Is that right?'

I smile modestly and say that yes, that's true.

'As you know, Alison, I've struggled with my weight myself in the past so I love it when someone else successfully loses weight. I must say that you're a very good advert for your own diet because you look fab.' Denise smiles and Jackie nods and agrees that I look *great.*

I feel the tension leave me slightly; I think they might like me.

'So, Alison.' Denise beams. 'Why don't you tell us a bit about *The Travis Way*?'

I launch into my practised spiel which by now I've done so often that I deliver it smoothly and I hope, convincingly. My nerves start to subside and I get to the end without messing up. Tarquin gives me a thumbs up from the other side of the studio.

'Thank you, Alison. I may even try it myself,' Denise says with a smile. We then have a couple of minutes of Jackie telling Denise that *she's gorgeous as she is and doesn't need to diet* and more sickening mutual compliments before Denise turns her attention to Warren.

'So, Warren, your book, *Cycling to Lose Weight*, was also flying off the shelves until quite recently, wasn't it?'

A small voice next to me mumbles. 'Yes.'

Jackie affects a puzzled expression.

'Warren, can you tell us, in your own words, why your book has now been withdrawn from sale?'

Warren mumbles something incomprehensible.

'Sorry?' Denise and Jackie look at each other and

smirk.

'I had a gastric band,' Warren bursts out. 'I didn't do any cycling, I would have done but I couldn't find a bike that could hold my weight. I do lots of cycling now I've lost the weight.'

The studio is silent and Denise and Jackie look at each other in mock astonishment. This is a favourite tactic of theirs and I've seen them use it many times.

'You mean...' Denise again turns to Jackie before facing the camera, 'You *lied?*'

'Well, I...'

Denise cuts across him, a look of outrage on her face.

'You let people pay fourteen pounds ninety-nine for a book that was a lie? You made people spend their hard earned cash on something that you *made up*?'

'I...'

'I don't know about our viewers but personally I find it *despicable* that you gave people hope that they could lose weight like you and it was all a complete fabrication.' Jackie shakes her head sadly.

Denise holds up her hand as if Jackie has gone too far; this is a favourite mannerism of hers which she uses just before they go in for the kill.

'Jackie, I'm sure Warren didn't *mean* to lie and he has lost a lot of weight, thirty stone isn't it, Warren?'

'Thirty-three,' Warren says, not seeing the trap that they've set for him.

'But that makes it worse, Denise,' Jackie announces, 'Because he's convinced other people that they can lose thirty-three stone by simply getting on a bike when really he had a *gastric band*.'

The last two words are said with absolute disgust and Denise nods her head sadly.

'Weight loss surgery, the easy, no will power way to lose weight, no effort at all,' Jackie goes on. 'The sort of surgery that your average dieter could never hope to afford.'

'But...' Warren tries to speak but Denise cuts across him.

'I think, Warren, that your actions speak for themselves, don't you agree, Alison?'

I nearly jump when she says my name and I stare at her.

'I'm sure you'll agree, Alison, that's there's a right and a wrong way to lose weight?'

'Oh, definitely.' I nod emphatically but it's not enough, the *Bold Women* want more.

'Wouldn't you agree, Alison, that Warren has been dishonest by unfairly *peddling* his book of lies and making money out of poor unassuming people who are absolutely desperate to lose weight?'

They're going in for the kill now and I say my practised answer that hopefully will come across to the viewers as me not agreeing with him but trying to be nice about it and not condemning him.

'I do agree, but I also feel sorry for Warren

because he was so desperate to lose weight that he had major surgery which I'm sure isn't very pleasant.'

Denise nods as if she agrees with me but there's a glint in her eye.

'I think you're being too nice, Alison. What do you think, Warren?'

All eyes are on Warren who squirms and says nothing, wishing for it to be over.

'Also.' Jackie grins. 'Weight loss surgery isn't without its problems, is it Warren? I've heard there was a rather unfortunate incident regarding a breakfast television sofa?'

Realisation and horror dawn on Warren's face and he turns so red I wonder if his head is going to explode.

'I believe you were there at the time, Alison, weren't you?' Jackie stares at me. 'Perhaps you could tell us about it as Warren is so unwilling.'

The bitches; they're going to make me do their dirty work for them which will make me look a complete cow too. Bile suddenly rises in my throat as I stare at Denise and Jackie and I swallow it down. Jackie and Denise have expressions on their faces that I've seen many times in my life although on this occasion they're directed at Warren and not me. Spiteful, sneering and bullying, the *I'm better/thinner/richer than you and that means I can humiliate you and you'll just have to sit there and take it.*

'You were sitting next to Warren, weren't you

Alison?' Jackie prompts.

'Yes. I was,' I say robotically.

'In your own words, Alison, what happened?'

There's an uncomfortable silence and I can see Tarquin across the studio waving his arms at me in an attempt to hurry me up.

'I have a confession to make.' I state in a flat voice, staring straight into the camera.

Denise and Jackie look at me and then each other, genuinely puzzled this time.

'A confession?' Jackie asks as I see Tarquin frantically waving his hands at me and making dramatic throat cutting gestures.

'Yes,' I hear myself say. 'My diet book is a complete lie, too.'

CHAPTER TEN

The whole of the studio erupted after I'd spoken, clipboards were hurriedly picked up, runners scurried and a hurried conversation was initiated with Tarquin by the grey haired man. None of this was helped by Warren somehow managing to fall from his precarious perch on his stool, taking it down with him in the process. He keeled over like a giant oak that had been chopped down and went down with such an almighty crash that the viewers couldn't fail to hear it even if the cameras weren't on him. Two of the runners scuttled over and helped pull him up from the floor while everyone else watched in gawping astonishment.

The most disconcerting thing was that Warren never took his eyes off me for the whole time it took him to fall and when he'd been manhandled and pulled back up to his feet he was gazing at me with something like wonder. The runners attempted to heave him back onto the stool but had to abandon that idea when they realised one of the legs was broken beyond repair and Warren was left to stand there like a lemon. He stood stock still like a statue in the place where the stool had been and would probably still be there now if we hadn't been hustled out of the studio.

Denise and Jackie never batted an eyelid when he fell despite the horrendous noise and I couldn't help feel a grudging respect for them; they might be a couple of bitches but they're true television professionals and absolutely nothing fazes them.

Denise carried on as nothing had happened and was staring at me with a shark-like smile. 'What exactly do you mean, Alison?'

This was when I realised that I *could* go back on what I'd said if I was clever about it; it was retrievable and I could talk my way out of it and back track and pretend that I'd got a bit mixed up. It was all quite do-able and there really wasn't any *need* to totally trash my career on live television. I did consider it for a brief moment but quickly realised that I didn't want to save my career.

'It's a lie,' I pronounced. Quite loudly too. 'The whole book is a complete lie, a load of made up nonsense. I looked at all of the popular diet plans on the internet and I simply cut and paste bits of them. *The Travis Way* is not how I lost weight at all.'

Denise and Jackie stared at me and for once they were lost for words and I know it wasn't in the slightest bit funny but I so wanted to burst out laughing and I'm not quite sure how I stopped myself.

'So *you* have a gastric band too?' Jackie demanded.

'God no.' I did laugh this time, I just couldn't help it and I realised with a shock that I was starting to enjoy myself immensely.

Jackie raised a micro-bladed eyebrow at me.

'Perhaps you'd like to explain yourself to our viewers.'

'Of course.' I paused for dramatic effect. 'The way I really lost weight was much simpler than a gastric band and absolutely anyone can do it and it's free, too. I starved myself and ate practically nothing, drank loads of black coffee and then ran around the streets every night for hours and hours until I nearly passed out.'

Denise and Jackie sat silently for several seconds; pantomime style mock horror plastered on their faces.

'You did what?' Denise asked in an attempt to make me incriminate myself further and I oblige.

'I starved myself and ran for hours and hours, simple as that.'

'So why didn't you put that in your book?' Denise demanded. 'Why lie about how you lost weight? Why not be *honest*?'

'Honest?' I chuckled. 'Because no one would buy a book like that, no one wants to starve themselves, do they? We have to dress it up and pretend that you can still pretty much eat what you want and do the absolute minimum in the way of exercise. Do you honestly think that anyone would *buy* a book with the truth in it?'

There was a moment silence while Jackie and Denise looked at each other with their outrage faces pasted on before Jackie rose to her feet.

'That's *despicable*!' she shouted at me. I'd been expecting this as I've seen her do this to many a victim on the show and then watched as the poor sap gabbled and grovelled in an attempt to justify themselves to her. I felt the weight of suspense in the studio as they waited for me to crumble.

'Isn't it just,' I said cheerfully.

A collective gasp ran around the studio and the surprise on Jackie's face was real this time and I found it all rather wonderful.

'That is disgusting,' Denise bellowed as she stood up and pointed her finger dramatically at me.

'Absolutely,' I agreed.

Jackie and Denise looked at each other in confusion and out of the corner of my eye I saw the grey haired man at the side of the studio making frantic cutting motions with his arms. Jackie pulled her gaze away from Denise and with her trademark wink smoothly informed the camera that *we'll be right back with you guys after a short break.*

So why did I do it? Why did I decide to tell the truth about *The Travis Way* on national television in front of millions of people when I didn't have to?

Why did I decide to tell the truth when I lie most of the time about almost everything?

I have no idea; maybe it was the thing with Blake playing on my mind – perhaps I took my eye off the ball, so to speak and slipped up? No, I don't think it was a slip up – I hadn't been planning to say it but when I did it was a deliberate act and it just felt so *right*. I opened my mouth and out it came; I hadn't planned it and I had no intention of doing it until I started speaking but once I'd started I felt exhilarated and free. It felt so good to say exactly what I was thinking instead of weighing each word carefully before I spoke to make sure that I wasn't making a blunder. And although I felt a bit sorry for Warren I didn't trash my entire career for him because I'm really not that nice.

Once we went to a commercial break they couldn't wait to get rid of me and I was pretty much frog marched out of the studio along with Warren. Tarquin tip tapped his way over to us and said we had to leave *immediately*.

'Why?' I asked innocently.

'You went off script,' he hissed at me whilst throwing a worried look at Denise and Jackie and I wondered if somehow he was going to get the blame. By the look on his face I think he was and that he knew it; the blame would be passed down from the top and settle squarely on his skinny shoulders because he was young, unimportant and completely dispensable. I'd wrong footed the stars of the show by going off script and they didn't like it; it was their show and I'd upstaged them by not grovelling or arguing with them. I'd agreed with what they were saying and that just wasn't acceptable; I was supposed to beg for their forgiveness for my heinous crime.

'Polly will take you back to collect your things and then you'll be escorted to the exit,' he snapped before he swivelled on his heels and marched over to stand in front of Jackie and Denise. I watched as he stood in front of them for a while and then slowly walked away after they totally ignored him and continued dissecting what had just happened between themselves. Yep, he's definitely getting the blame.

Perky blonde Polly bounced over to us but there was no jaunty smile or greeting this time, she simply stopped in front of us with her clipboard and marched off, expecting us to follow. I did consider not moving for a moment and making it difficult for her and Denise and Jackie but then thought better of it; you can push your luck too far and I think Warren was ready to pass out by then so we followed her across the floor and out into the maze of corridors.

I couldn't stop laughing, particularly when I looked over at Denise and Jackie's pinched, annoyed faces as we left. I gave them a cheery little wave and although I'm sure they saw me they didn't wave back or even acknowledge me.

I thought Polly had walked quickly on the way in but she practically ran as we wended our way through the winding corridors to the green room. Warren and I gave up trying to keep up after a while and when she finally noticed we weren't behind her she had to come back for us and slow down. Once we'd been deposited in the green room Polly stood guard over us while we gathered up our coats and belongings. She then escorted us downstairs to Reception where she had a brief, whispered conversation with the uniformed security guard before disappearing back to the studio without even a *goodbye*. The security guard had nodded and looked very serious as she was speaking and when she'd finished he strode over to us and said we had to *vacate the premises NOW*. He was full of self-importance and swagger and loomed over us as we walked to the revolving doors. Once outside he followed behind us and stood watching as we walked along the street, just in case we made an attempt to get back in. I think it probably made his day because he seemed to be enjoying it all far too much.

Warren and I trundled around to the back alley behind the television centre and when we got to the car park Warren asked me if I needed a lift and I said no thanks, because I had a car and driver waiting for me – probably for the last time as I'd pretty much blown up my whole career. But I couldn't even feel bad about it; no doubt the media will give me a good slagging off for a week or two but this time next month I'll be old news and someone else will be in the firing line. Shockingly, as we stood there Warren suddenly threw his arms around me and hugged me extremely tightly and thanked me. He was a bit sweaty and had a strange smell of pickled onions about him so I had to hold my breath for a while.

'What?' I said, awkwardly extricating myself from the unasked for and unwanted hug. 'Are you thanking me for?'

'For sticking up for me, for sticking together and stopping them from humiliating me in front of the entire world.'

I thought he was being a bit over dramatic because whilst *Bold Women* has good viewing figures it's hardly the whole world, and did he really imagine that I'd done it for him?

I could have put him right of course but I decided not to tell him he was wrong - because why spoil someone's illusion that you're a nice person? What's to be gained from being honest about that – it's not as if it would change anything, so I smiled in what I hoped was an enigmatic way, wished him well for the future and bid him farewell before he got any ideas about us being friends or anything sad like that.

It's done now and there's no going back; I've had my five minutes of fame and now I can disappear back into obscurity and have a bit of peace. I never had any intentions of writing a diet book or being famous and it all happened by accident so I don't feel as if I've lost anything important because I never actually wanted it in the first place.

Besides which I didn't exactly lose it, it wasn't accidental; I quite deliberately threw it away.

I feel quite relieved now that it's all over and I have more than enough money of my own to live on and also now that I'm getting married I don't need a job because I'm going to be a housewife; and maybe I could take some cookery lessons because I don't think Gerald's the sort to eat a microwave meal or pork chops and mash.

Oh God, that's reminded me, what's Gerald going to say?

I've lied to him too and I don't know how he's going to feel about that – I know he's besotted with me for some strange reason but I'm sure there's only so much lying he can take because he's a truthful type of person himself. I don't want to use up all of my *get out of jail free* cards too quickly and especially not before the wedding. Maybe I should have waited until I got the ring on my finger before I decided to come over all honest.

Too late now; although I'm fairly confident that I'll be able to talk him round, I might have to squeeze a few tears out and tell him how ashamed I feel, although actually I don't.

I feel liberated.

* * *

As we headed out of London in the car, Aiden phoned me constantly but I ignored his calls and turned my phone to silent to get some peace and quiet. There's no way that I can bear to talk to him at the moment as he's annoying enough when everything is going well so God knows what he'll be like now.

I haven't heard from Gerald so I'm guessing he hasn't seen *Bold Women* and doesn't know anything about it, he'll be busy beavering away at work doing solicitor type things. Should I tell him now before Aiden tells him - if he hasn't already? I think I should, it won't go down very well if he hears the news from someone else. I decide to send him a brief text and say that I'll explain when I see him.

Darling, I need to talk to you re The Travis Way – I think I've been rather silly but please don't be cross xx

Suitably vague and a bit gushing but I think it'll do. Doris must have been watching the show as it went out live because I had a text from her before I'd even got into the car.

Wtf? Call me!!!

I couldn't think what to reply so I sent an embarrassed looking emoji and left it at that. I hadn't even considered the ramifications for Doris – her nice new job will be gone because no one's going to want to buy the book now, are they? There won't be any need for any more road shows or promotions. And there's nothing I can do about that because the truth is out of the box and it won't be going back in. I could ask Gerald to put a word in with one of his friends and they could give her a job or maybe Aiden will find her something because he definitely has the hots for her. I'm sure I'll be able to sort something out because it's not her fault and there's no reason why she should suffer.

Seamus the driver kept asking me questions about my appearance on *Bold Women* which he doesn't normally do - usually it's a quick *everything go well*? And that's it. Which tells me that he must have watched it on his phone or maybe it's on the internet already. I was very non-committal and just said it was fine because I need to think how I'm going to handle this – not blurt out the first thing I fancy saying, like I did on *Bold Women.* I certainly won't be doing a Warren and going on television trying to justify myself or apologising to the public; no chance. I might go to a health spa for a couple of weeks and come back when it's all blown over and I'm yesterday's news. I'll take Doris with me as a consolation prize for not having her job anymore and she can have lots of treatments; she'd love it. Although we'd have to have separate rooms because I couldn't stand twenty-four hours a day of her, I'd have to have some respite.

My vague answers didn't stop Seamus from constantly asking questions and he kept on fishing so I put my head back and closed my eyes and pretended to be asleep just to shut him up. And of course the minute I'd done that I felt my phone vibrate and when I sneaked a look it was Aiden. His message was brief, but to the point:

2:45 this afternoon, Langans, table at the rear out of sight

Which is just over an hour away. He obviously knows that I'm not going to answer the phone to him and he must be really mad because he's fitting me in today although he's always droning on about how important and busy he is. Typically he thinks he can order me around even though I employ *him* and assumes that I'll do as I'm told and meet him. He also knows that I'm already in London so I can't lie and say I can't get there in time.

He only wants to meet so that he can tell me that he no longer wants to handle my PR – which he could do over the phone but he obviously thinks he can make me squirm and then bill me for an overpriced meal in the process. He'll drone on in his tedious manner about what a mess I've made of everything and how I didn't follow his plan. Honestly, I could die of boredom just thinking about it.

I'm sorely tempted to reply and tell him that I'm not coming. I don't need to sit and listen to his robotic moaning about what a fool I've made of myself and how I've ruined any future book sales. I already know it and I don't see why I should have to listen to him telling me off. I start to reply saying I'm not coming but change my mind; I've quite enjoyed telling the truth for a change so maybe I'll tell him a few truths about himself and get in first and sack him before he says he can't work for me anymore. I look at my watch; half past one – I'll have to tell Seamus to turn around and head back into London when we're barely got out of the centre. Maybe I'll have a couple of drinks if I'm early; I think I deserve one.

And I won't be having salad either.

Ok see you at 2.45 I text, and just for devilment I add an emoji crying with laughter.

As Doris would say; *suck on that, Aiden.*

* * *

I've ordered a very expensive bottle of wine as a sort of celebration and am starting my second glass of wine by the time Aiden arrives. The first glass of wine slipped down okay but if I'm completely honest I'm not enjoying it that much and I wish I'd stuck to my usual cheaper bottle.

I've studied the menu and I'm going to have lasagne which is one of my favourite meals but I *never* have it because it's so calorific. I might even have garlic bread to go with it. I still haven't heard anything from Gerald and when I checked he hadn't even read my message so he must be in a super important, boring meeting. I'm feeling a bit anxious about it and veer between thinking he'll call the engagement off and telling myself not to be so stupid. Would he really not want to marry me because I lied about how I lost weight?

Aiden appears at the table in his usual silent manner and I look up at him, tip my glass of wine in a salute to him and raise an eyebrow, I just can't help myself. He sits down opposite me and summons the waiter with a flick of a skinny white finger and orders a Caesar salad and a mineral water without even consulting the menu or speaking to me. When the waiter asks what I want for some reason I order a Caesar salad too; I'm not feeling hungry at all, maybe it's the telling off that I'm about to receive although I really couldn't give a hoot what he thinks.

Aiden gives me a long level look and then leans across the table towards me; the better to give me a roasting I assume.

'So. Bold Women.'

I say nothing but take another sip of the wine. Yuk, I definitely won't be ordering that one again; more expensive isn't always better - or maybe it's corked. I take another sip; yep, definitely corked. Aiden continues to stare at me, his nostrils flaring. I'm not going to answer him and make it easy for him. If he's waiting for me to explain he'll be waiting for a very long time. Besides, I can't even explain it to myself, never mind him.

'What made you do it?' he asks in his monotonous, boring drone.

'Don't know.' I say jauntily although I don't feel jaunty. I feel deflated and flat now the excitement is over and I only have explanations and grovelling to look forward to. I really can't be bothered with it all. He continues to stare at me and eventually I give in.

'Seemed like a good idea at the time.' I shrug.

I watch as he breathes in through his nose, only his flared nostrils betraying the fact that he's actually alive and not a clone of a real person. At least I won't have to see *his* annoying face anymore which is another huge positive to having blown up my career.

'Alison,' he announces solemnly, 'I have to say that it was a brilliant move, an absolute masterstroke that even I would never have dared to attempt.'

'What?' I splutter, wine nearly spraying over the table.

'Before the commercial break was even over I had every major tabloid on the phone wanting to interview you. Not to mention both BBC and ITV wanting you back on their breakfast shows.'

I think about this for a moment.

'That'll be so they can humiliate me, I suppose, like *Bold Women* were going to do with Warren?'

Aiden waves his hand in a dismissive manner. 'I don't think so but it doesn't matter – you're vastly different to Warren. But no, I don't think they want to bring you down – they're loving your honesty and they're half in love with you already because of your attendance at the Women of the Year awards.'

I stare at him wide-eyed.

'For some reason they seem to think that you have class,' he adds, as if this is something he can't even begin to understand.

'But how is it being honest if I've ripped people off by selling them a book that's a bunch of lies.'

Aiden makes that peculiar snorting noise which passes for a laugh.

'Diet book sales don't depend on truth, they never have. If anything it'll probably give sales a bit of a boost. No, there's no such thing as bad publicity and this is definitely *good*.'

I twirl the wine around in my glass thoughtfully. I don't agree about there being no such thing as bad publicity because look at Warren but he seems very sure of what he's saying and although I hate him, Aiden does know his stuff. Strangely, he hasn't once asked about the real way I lost weight; just not interested, I suppose.

'You've surprised me, Alison.' He sits back and studies me as if I were an exhibit in a museum and stretches his face into a facsimile of a smile.

'To be honest, I think your media career is just beginning. This is just the start, who knows where it could go from here.'

I'm in shock; I thought I'd killed my career dead and now he's telling me that I've actually improved it. As the waiters bring our salads and arrange them in front of us my brain is whirling with visions of more television appearances and book signings and staged events and it's suddenly very clear to me why I did what I did.

I don't want it; I don't want any of it.

I just want it all to be over.

CHAPTER ELEVEN

After the meal with Aiden – which, incidentally I didn't eat, so the worry diet definitely works as I think I was subconsciously fretting about explaining myself to Gerald – Seamus drove me straight home and I waited for Gerald to arrive. I had planned on popping out in my car to the big Tesco's to buy some binge food but I didn't bother so this subconscious worrying must be bad. I paced around the apartment and generally got on my own nerves until Gerald finally texted me at about seven o'clock to say that his meeting was finished and he was on his way over.

That was all the text said, no indication of how he felt about anything. I had no idea whether he was coming to tell me it was all over between us or if he was going to forgive me.

And as it's turned out he says there's absolutely nothing to forgive and that everything is all his fault – yes, he really said that. The way he sees it is that he was the one who talked me into writing the book in the first place and then insisted on getting Aiden involved. He says that he didn't listen to me and swept me along with the whole thing without considering what *I* wanted. He declared that I'm far too nice and that I need to be more insistent about what I want and not try to please everyone else. He feels an absolute brute for pushing me into something that I didn't want to do and he's furious with himself for not really giving me a choice about any of it. He's insistent that the blame should sit squarely on his shoulders even though I protested that it really *wasn't* his fault but mine; I didn't protest too much though because why look a gift horse in the mouth?

So now we're sitting on the sofa and I've managed to squeeze a few tears out in between telling Gerald that it's not his fault at all and also how *awful* I feel about people buying my book when it's a big lie.

I don't really feel awful.

People expect you to cry, don't they? Somehow it confirms that you're genuinely feeling as bad as you say you are. The last time that I cried was when I got arrested and Gerald came to my rescue – tears were *absolutely* required then so that Gerald could play the part of my knight in shining armour. Aside from that I can't recall when I last turned on the waterworks, as Mother used to call them. Mother had no time for crying of any description; a silent tear rolling down my cheek or a full on snotty sob elicited the same reaction - a stinging slap across the face followed by a long spell in the cellar. I learned this fact very early on in life and so became very adept at holding back the tears no matter how awful I might have been feeling.

Gerald gently wipes a tear from my face with his thumb and brushes my hair back from my face.

'My poor darling, you must tell me what you want to do.'

'Do?' I say in my best *being brave* voice.

'Well, do you want to carry on with Aiden and your marketing or do you just want to call a halt to the whole thing? Put it all behind you and forget any of it ever happened?'

I desperately want to put it all behind me and never have to mention or even think about *The Travis Way* ever again and that's exactly what I had intended doing but Aiden seems to think that it won't be that easy.

'I want to put a stop to the whole thing but Aiden says that's not a good idea.'

'Aiden? When did you see Aiden? Gerald looks slightly annoyed and maybe a teensy bit jealous and I see that I'm going to have to be careful, Gerald has no idea that I've had a meeting with Aiden because he assumed that he'd be the first person I'd call.

'This afternoon. He rang me on the way home from *Bold Women* and said I had to meet him. You know what Aiden's like, he was very insistent although I really didn't want to go - I just wanted to get home to you, darling.'

I sniff bravely and Gerald puts his arm around me and pulls me closer.

'I'm here now, sweetheart, don't you worry. Aiden had no right badgering you and I'll be having words with him when I see him, I'm sure he could have waited. Why was it so urgent?'

'He said that since the show aired he's been bombarded with calls from the media about it and they were clamouring for interviews with me. Well, I told him that I wanted to finish with the promotion and everything and keep a low profile but he says that's the very worst thing I could do and that it wouldn't go down well with the public.'

To say Aiden was shocked when I told him I'd had enough would be an understatement; he couldn't understand why I didn't want to carry on and make loads more money out of it. He said I could pretty much name my price right now but it wouldn't be that way for very long; I needed to strike while the iron was hot. He made it very clear that if I thought I could vanish and live a quiet life again then I was very much mistaken. He said I'd be hounded by the press and on social media and my life wouldn't be worth living. No, he said, I'd started something and I had to finish it, whether I wanted to or not. I don't know whether he was lying and the truth was that he didn't want his cash cow disappearing before he'd fully milked her but can I really afford to take that chance?

Gerald looks thoughtful.

'What feeling did he get from the media? Were they wanting you for interviews so they could do a hatchet job on you?'

'Aiden didn't seem to think so. He said that they liked that I'd been so outspoken. He seemed to think that there was a very positive spin on what I'd said and it could work to my advantage.'

'Hmm...' Gerald says thoughtfully, 'In which case he might have a point. The public expect and all that - and Aiden does know his stuff, so if he's saying that you can't just disappear then he's probably right.'

'He said that it wasn't just interviews they wanted but other stuff too. Apparently *Tellytalk* were one of the first to ring him; he got the impression from them that there's an open chequebook if I'd agree to do a series with them.'

'Tellytalk?' Gerald roars with laughter. 'What? A programme where people watch people watching television and then talk drivel about it! Good God, as if you'd go on that; God only knows what sort of people watch *that* sort of rubbish.'

Me. I'm the sort that watches that sort of rubbish and I love it actually, not that I'll be telling Gerald that anytime soon. When Aiden said it I did think that if I *have* to do some stuff to get the media off my back I might very well do

Tellytalk because I wouldn't have to talk about me and my non diet – I could talk about television programmes which I'm a bit of an expert on – and it's pre-recorded so they can edit out bits that I don't like.

'*We're Watching You* was mentioned, too.'

'Was it? I didn't realise it was still going, thought it had finished years ago. Surely you wouldn't want to spend a week in *the mansion* with a bunch of Z list celebrities?'

So Gerald *has* watched that. I thought it had finished too but apparently they announce that every series is the last because it bumps the viewing figures up. I definitely wouldn't do that show no matter how much money they offered; I might not be a very nice person but I don't think I'd last five minutes in that mansion. And depending how they edit it they can make the nicest people appear to be psychopaths so God knows how I'd come across. And actually, from what I've seen some of the people on there really *are* psychopaths so why would I possibly want to put myself through that?

'Do you agree with Aiden that I have to carry on?' I ask.

'No, not if you really don't want to but you should give it some serious thought before you make a decision. And if you do decide to give it a go be selective in what you decide to do. Maybe you could get away with doing a few interviews and then hopefully a new bit of scandal will come along and you'll be yesterdays news.'

I say nothing but close my eyes and relax into Gerald's shoulder. I feel absolutely shattered and I wish he would go so that I could just go to sleep. But realistically there's no chance of that because I'll have to give Gerald some of my time as he's being so understanding and taking the blame for everything but honestly, I'm completely talked out and my head is spinning with so much to think about.

Gerald-wise it seems as if I can do no wrong and if it wasn't for the Blake thing hanging over me I'd be as happy as Larry, whoever he is. I can stomach doing the required amount of television appearances and newspaper interviews before the media lose interest in me and I disappear back into anonymity but the Blake problem isn't going to go away so easily.

Why is it that when almost everything is going so well in my life there's always something or someone to spoil it? Having finally got away from Mother I thought I'd never be in this position again but now Blake has come along and is going to spoil it all if I'm not very careful.

'I don't know about you but I could definitely do with a drink – glass of wine darling? Shall I make us a sandwich?' Gerald says as he gently takes his arms from around me and gets up from the sofa.

'Glass of wine sounds lovely but I'm really not hungry,' I say as he heads to the kitchen, which is a lie because I don't want anything to drink I just want him to leave so I can flop into bed. On my own. Also, he's going to have trouble making anything in my kitchen because the cupboards are completely bare. I open my mouth to tell him and then close it again; I really don't have the energy and he'll find out for himself soon enough.

'Now darling, you're not still doing this silly starving business, are you?'

'Of course not,' I say. 'I had a meal earlier when I met Aiden at *The Langan*.'

'Oh, I didn't realise you'd had a meal with him.'

There's that flash of jealousy again and I realise I've slipped up again. God, this lying and keeping people happy is exhausting.

'Well I did tell you we had a meeting, didn't I? It was his suggestion to meet at *The Langan* and seeing as it's a restaurant it would have seemed churlish to sit there and eat nothing just to make a point. Aiden is handling all of my PR and considering the fool I'd just made of myself on *Bold Women* you must see why I couldn't really get out of it.'

'Of course you'd couldn't, darling, absolutely not,' Gerald says hurriedly. 'Don't think for one minute that I'm blaming you.'

I'm not quite sure what I'm not getting blamed for so I say nothing and Gerald resumes his journey to the kitchen.

'Good God, what's that?'

Gerald stops in front of the bookcase and stares up at the ugly pottery bird that's sitting on the top shelf. It ended up there because I couldn't find anywhere else to put it. I moved it around the room but it didn't look right anywhere and the bookcase was the last resort before it got flung into the bin. It peers down at us from on high with a disgusted look on its face looking very much like Mother.

Gerald moves closer to the bookcase to get a better view.

'Where on earth did you get it?'

'It was my father's,' I say. 'I found it in his crate of belongings from the nursing home.'

Gerald nods slowly. 'It's...interesting.'

'It's ugly,' I say, 'But it's the only thing that I have of my father's so I thought I should keep some kind of memento of him even though I never had the opportunity to meet him.'

'Hmm...' Gerald picks up the bird from the bookcase and brings it down to study it more closely. He frowns and turns it around in his hands.

'For some reason it looks very familiar.'

It definitely looks like Mother but Gerald never met her so he can't possibly mean her. I hope to God I'm not starting to look like her although it would probably serve me right for being so horrible; sort of poetic justice.

'I'm sure it'll come back to me.'

He places it carefully back up on the shelf and continues his journey out to the kitchen. Suddenly wide awake I jump up from the sofa and walk over and stand in front of the huge mirror hanging over the wall unit. I press my face up close and scrutinise my reflection, I turn my head to the left and then to the right and back again.

Am I?

Am I starting to look like Mother?

I finally pleaded a headache at about half past nine; I didn't really have a headache but I *was* very tired and I didn't know how much longer I could keep up the *nice me* act. Gerald's an absolute sweetheart and a saint, actually, there's absolutely no doubt about it but enough is enough, for God's sake.

As soon as he'd gone I brushed my teeth and flopped into bed and then found that typically, I couldn't sleep. After tossing and turning for a while I gave up trying and sat up and put the television on and channel hopped until I found an old, unthreatening film to watch in the hope that it would help me drift off.

Then I thought that I'd better text Doris back because she'd be worrying about her job so I should do the right thing and put her mind at rest. Also, she'd texted me about ten times since *Bold Women* and I didn't want her texting me all night. Honestly, some people are so needy. I'd just picked up my mobile to text her and it rang in my hand, *Doris*, flashing up as the caller. I turned the volume down on the television and pressed the button and answered it before I changed my mind; might as well get it over with and then maybe I could get some peace.

'Hi, Doris.'

'At last! You okay?' She carries right on without waiting for an answer. 'Aiden said you wanted to stop the book and everyfink. He finks you're mad.'

I don't say anything and the silence stretches until Doris finally breaks it.

'Well? You still doing fings or not?"

'I'm still thinking about it,' I say. How dare Aiden talk about me to Doris, that's not what I pay him for. 'When did you speak to him?'

'Couple of hours ago. He was dead impressed wiv the way you handled those two bitches and a bit pissed off that it wasn't his idea. I fink he only rang me to let me know my job was safe in case I was worrying about it, said he'd find me somefing else if you decided to bail out.'

Bloody cheek. I know he's got the hots for Doris but who does he think he is telling her what we've discussed? I'll definitely be having words with him and they won't be nice ones.

'So are you?'

'What?'

'Stopping the book and all the promo?'

I let the question hang for a few minutes just to make Doris suffer although realistically I have no choice. If I don't want to be hounded by the gutter press I'll have to make a few token appearances at least.

'Of course not,' I eventually say. 'I just have to decide what to do, discuss with Aiden which is the best way to go.'

'Fank fuck for that,' Doris says with relief. 'This is the best job I've ever had and I don't want to lose it even though Aiden said he'd get me another I'd rather work wiv you.'

I can't blame her for thinking about herself but really, does she have to be so obvious about it?

'But you 'ave to do what's best for you,' she adds as if reading my mind. I make a non-committal noise and wonder how I can get her off the phone so I can try and go to sleep. I decide honesty's the best policy.

'Anyway, Doris, I'm a bit worn out after the day I've had so I'm going to go now. I'll speak to you tomorrow.'

'Okay Al, no probs. Just promise me one fing.'

'What?'

'Fink about doing *We're Watching You* cos I fucking love that programme.'

* * *

Wednesday and Thursday passed uneventfully and luckily Gerald was really busy with work so I haven't seen him since Tuesday night, although he's phoned and texted me constantly. I've also managed to avoid Aiden as I told him that I've got some sort of bug; which isn't a complete lie because I don't feel very well at all. I have absolutely no energy and strangely, no appetite. Aiden has very graciously allowed me the rest of the week off before we start the book promotion again because the very fact that I'm not in a rush to justify myself to the media has ramped my price up a bit more. On Monday I have an interview with a women's top celebrity magazine as they want to run a centre spread on me. Aiden has said I can basically say what I want instead of him telling me what to say - but what else is there to say? I lied and that's it, basically. I also have an interview with the producers of *Tellytalk* although I'm not sure about that because that sort of thing could run and run and I'd never be able to disappear then, so maybe I'll turn it down if they offer it to me. Maybe I could act a bit dumb and then they won't want me. Although realistically the *Tellytalk* bar isn't set very high to start with so acting dumb wouldn't prevent them from wanting me on the show.

Anyway, I'm not worrying about any of that now because I have the more pressing problem of Blake and how to get rid of him. I've agreed to meet him at the car park again because that worked quite well last time. He doesn't know it but there's no way I'm giving him ten grand, he's getting five and no more. Apart from anything else I can't just swan into the bank and draw ten thousand pounds out, can I? I'm sure there'd be questions asked although I've never actually tried getting that much. Would I have to give them notice to draw out a large amount of cash? I have no idea and I'd made my mind up that if I couldn't get five thousand Blake would just have to put up with whatever I was allowed to withdraw.

I felt quite conspicuous asking for five thousand pounds cash and before I got there I was certain that I was going to be questioned as to what I wanted the money for. I made up lots of reasons in my head in advance and finally settled on paying a builder for a house extension. By the time I got into the bank I'd changed my mind and decided that if I was asked I was just going to ignore them. It's my money and I don't need to justify myself to anyone. And the cashier didn't ask anyway, she could barely look at me let alone speak to me or engage me in any sort of conversation as she handed over the five thousand pounds without even asking me what denomination notes I wanted. I was a bit peeved to be honest; I have a lot of money in that bank and frankly, they could be a bit nicer when they serve me.

So, Blake can have the five thousand *after* he's given me all of the photographs and if he won't give them to me then I'll just have to go to the police and take the consequences from Gerald. I can't live with the Blake thing hanging over me and if I have to keep paying him I'll have no money left. I need him out of my life forever before Gerald and I get married.

I've arrived ten minutes early and as I walk up to the ticket machine I can see he's already there waiting - fortunately there's no one else around to witness our meeting. I've taken the precaution of not parking in this car park but using the one behind the precinct because I didn't want to chance bumping into him as I was parking my car. No doubt he'd have hung around my car waiting for me to get out even though I've told him not to *ever* approach me or acknowledge that he knows me.

I've also taken the precaution of dressing in jeans, trainers and a dark blue hoodie with the hood pulled up over my hair instead of my usual designer wear. I daren't take the chance of someone recognising me and I don't know if Blake has arranged for an undesirable mate to hang around watching and possibly snapping photographs. Though realistically I don't think he'd want to share the money or the secret with anyone else.

He grins cockily as I walk up to him and I notice that he has a brand new suit on which definitely isn't a Foodco special. Also he's wearing shiny, expensive looking leather shoes so he's obviously spent the thousand pounds already and anticipates lots more. I stop and stand about three feet away from him.

'Not in a hurry today, doll?' I take it he's referring to the last time when I practically threw the money at him and vanished. He clacks grey gum around his mouth and I avert my eyes from the disgusting spectacle as my stomach rolls and bile rises in my throat.

'I need to speak to you before I give you the money.'

'Just hand it over doll, I ain't in the mood.' The gum clacks even harder.

He's about to speak again but I hold my hand up to stop him.

'I'm not just handing it over, you can have it when you've deleted the photo and any others that you took.' I won't tell him it's not ten thousand because once I've got the photographs what can he do about it? I could have just put a thousand in the envelope or nothing at all now I come to think of it. I've not been thinking straight which is hardly surprising with the week I've had; to say Aiden has been keeping on at me is an understatement.

'Oh, yeah?' He sneers. 'I don't think so, I ain't stupid. There's no way you'll pay me once you've got them.'

'I will. I promise. I'm a woman of my word.'

He eyes scan my face, trying to detect if I'm lying; if he can trust me.

'No. I want the whole ten grand first then I'll delete the photo.'

So there is only one.

'No. No more money until you've deleted it.'

'Please yourself, doll.' He shrugs. 'I'll go to the papers or *Bold Women*, I'm sure they'd like to hear all about our affair, cos actually, I think ten grand is a bit *cheap* considering how famous you are now.'

I stare at him and he smirks, convinced that he has the upper hand.

'Okay, please yourself. I thought I've give you

a chance before I go to the police but you leave me no option.' I turn to leave because I've realised that he's never going to stop and my only option is to come clean and probably lose Gerald in the process. I don't care; I just want to go home and lie down and go to sleep.

'The police?' There's a different tone in his voice now, not quite so cocky.

'Yes, the police, because you're blackmailing me and that's a criminal offence.'

He chews the gum even harder as his pea sized brain tries to calculate whether I'm bluffing or not. His eyes narrow and he lunges towards me to try and grab the envelope in my hand but I see what he's about to do and thrust my hand into his chest and roughly push him away. If he's not deleting the photo he's definitely not getting the money.

'Photo first then you can have the money.'

He doesn't answer but makes a strange whistling noise and looks at me in a surprised sort of way and his mouth opens and closes putting me in mind of a fish that's just been landed in a net. I'm about to ask him what he's playing at when it slowly dawns on me that Blake is choking. He's no longer clacking the grey gum around his mouth and I assume it has somehow lodged in his throat and he can neither swallow it nor spit it out. Gasping for breath, he puts out a hand towards me in a grasping manner and I step back smartly to avoid him touching me.

He waves one hand at me and clutches his

throat with the other as he tries in vain to breathe in and I can see the panic in his eyes. Should I attempt the Heimlich manoeuvre? I don't know exactly how to do it but I'm sure I could have a stab at it because I've seen it re-enacted a few times on TV.

Or do I walk away and let him choke to death?

It's a dilemma, isn't it?

CHAPTER TWELVE

I'm going to be late for my interview with Woman Today because I just couldn't seem to drag myself out of bed. Gerald has been going on at me all weekend to see a doctor because this bug seems to be lasting so long and I can't seem to shake it off. I felt so rough that we had to cancel our planned engagement ring shopping – I was so disappointed but also immensely relieved because I felt so ill.

Gerald was so worried that he wanted to call a doctor out to me and I only prevented him from doing so by promising that I'd make an appointment first thing this morning if I wasn't feeling better. He was beginning to majorly get on my nerves about it and I know it's only because he's concerned, but every time I looked at him all I could see was his mouth moving and I just wanted him to *shut up* and leave me alone.

Which set me to thinking that when we're married there'd be no getting away from him and I'd be trapped like I was with Mother, because I can hardly lock him upstairs in a bedroom can I? Am I making a massive mistake by getting married to him? I thought about it and came to the conclusion that it would most likely be fine because he goes to work every day so it wouldn't be twenty-four-seven like it was with Mother. He quite often works late too, so I think I'll be able to tolerate his *going on* for weekends and evenings because it won't be much different from now. Although I do wonder whether I'm cut out to be married and living with someone else because I have a very low tolerance level.

This bit of light soul searching developed into a whole chain of *am I doing the right thing* thinking which made my headache even worse so I've had to not think about it along with all of the other things that I'm not thinking about. And believe me, trying to not think about things is almost as exhausting as actually thinking about them. In the end I had to tell *myself* to shut up; mentally, obviously because I haven't actually started talking to myself out loud. If Mother was here she could have given me a slap around the face and that would have sorted me out. Anyway, I suppose I can always get a divorce if he really drives me mad.

Although I've assured Gerald that if I don't feel

better soon I'll definitely see a doctor I think that the events of last week probably have more to do with how I'm feeling than anything physical; a type of delayed shock. Or maybe I've got an incurable illness; payback for being horrible, God's revenge for being a very bad person. I do try to be better but things just keep happening that make me do awful things.

Anyway, I don't believe in God. Or Santa Claus. Never have done and surely you have to *believe* for God's revenge to work.

See what I mean? Just *shut up* Alison.

By the time I eventually get myself outside to the car Seamus has been waiting for a good half-hour. It's taken me forever to drag myself out of the shower and slap some make-up on to try and make myself look anywhere near presentable. The make-up actually makes me look worse and I would have wiped it all off again but that would have taken even longer, plus I really couldn't be bothered.

I flop down into the back seat of the car like a sack of potatoes. I wish I could time travel and transport myself to this afternoon and back to the comfort of my bed.

'Late one, was it?' Seamus says with a smirk, looking at me in the mirror as we pull away from the kerb.

Thanks; if there was any doubt at all that I don't look like shit, Seamus has just dispelled it. I could have cancelled the interview and rescheduled it for another time but I just want it out of the way and over and done with.

'Something like that,' I say.

He grins in the mirror and in no time at all we're zooming up the motorway to London. Once we get into London centre the stop and start nature of the driving starts to make me feel queasy and I press the button to roll down the window. A blast of car fumes billow into the car and I quickly close it again. Just as I'm about to ask Seamus to pull over and stop somewhere so I can get out we pull into the side of the road and come to a halt. It seems we've arrived.

The interview is being conducted in a trendy little restaurant in Kensington rather than the magazine's offices. I've told the journalist that I won't require lunch, just drinks; no alcohol either because I can't face it.

Seamus parks the car on the pavement outside *Bistro Beach*, a tall, narrow, bay fronted terrace that looks more like someone's house than a restaurant. As I step onto the pavement and look at the place I half expect to see net curtains hanging in the windows. I tell Seamus to pick me up in exactly one hour although he suggests that I ring him and let him know when I'm finished, rather than setting a time limit but I say no, exactly one hour. I have absolutely no intention of staying any longer than I have to. Seamus doesn't like this and persists in trying to make me ring him when I'm done. I'm pretty sure he's got plans and if we go with his idea I'll be waiting around while he finishes whatever he's doing before he comes and gets me. He's getting a bit above himself, if you ask me, with his snide remarks about my appearance and trying to tell me what to do. I think he's forgetting he's just the driver. I've barely shut the car door before he zooms off in a temper to show his displeasure, nearly running over my foot in the process.

I trudge up the steps to the restaurant entrance and enter through the bright yellow painted door into a room that looks like it belongs more at the seaside than the centre of London. Small tables with brightly coloured tablecloths and deckchair type seats; there are red tin buckets in the middle of the tables full of knives and forks. A smiling waiter wearing a Hawaiian shirt approaches me and asks if I've booked a table. I stop myself from asking if it matters because the restaurant is completely empty save for one table at the back of the room where a lone female is sitting. No lunch time rush here. I give him my name and tell him that I'm meeting someone. He nods enthusiastically and walks down the room and I follow him. His feet make a peculiar flapping sound as he walks and I look down to see that he has flip flops on to go with the Hawaiian shirt and below the knee shorts. The flip flops reveal hairy troll-like feet with over long toe nails; a theme is all very well but those feet are going to put the most committed diner off their food – no wonder the place is empty.

'Hi, Alison.' Susie Petherbridge stands up and

puts her hand out and we shake hands. For some reason I was expecting someone much older but she's about my age, or maybe even younger. Dressed in jeans and a huge baggy jumper she peers at me through glasses that magnify her eyes to owl like proportions.

I sit down opposite her and once the waiter has taken my order for a mineral water he flaps off.

'Can't I tempt you to lunch?' Susie asks.

'No, I'm fine,' I assure her. 'But don't let me stop you.'

She doesn't, either. When the waiter returns with my drink she orders spaghetti Bolognese with a side order of garlic bread and I'm guessing it's all going on expenses. It seems the disgusting hairy feet aren't putting her off her food. I realise I'm going to feel awkward watching her eat while I sit there with nothing so I order a bowl of chicken soup with some bread. If I nibble on the dry bread it might make me feel a bit better.

'Shall we make a start now or do you want to wait until after?'

'Now's fine.'

She places a small recorder on the table and turns it on.

'Okay. I'm going to ask you some questions but when I write the article up it'll be written as if we've had a cosy chat, not a formal Q and A, are you okay with that?'

'Yes, that's fine.'

'Okie dokie. So, first of all, your book, *The Travis*

Way, I understand that it's still flying off the shelves and that your outburst on *Bold Women* has actually *increased* sales?'

'That's right,' I say, because amazingly, it has. Although if she's going to ask questions like this that only require two word answers I don't think we're going to get very far.

'Is it really true that you wrote your book by cutting and pasting bits off of the internet?'

'Yes.'

'So what prompted you to confess on *Bold Women*? Did you plan to reveal all before you agreed to appear?'

Aiden told me that this is going to be a question that everyone will ask and I've given it a lot of thought. Apparently if I say it was a spur of the moment thing it'll devalue what I did; he said that I need to make it look as if it was a considered decision to come clean and stop defrauding the public.

More lying.

And I can't do it.

'No.'

'No?' She looks surprised. 'Oh, that wasn't the impression I got from Aiden.'

So much for being allowed to say what I want; Aiden has clearly briefed her on what's to be expected from me.

'Really?' I raise an eyebrow. 'You've spoken to him, have you?'

'Um, yes. I've known Aiden for years, we were at

uni together.'

Another one of his cronies, although I wouldn't have guessed because she doesn't look as old as him although actually now I look at her properly I can barely see her face for the massive glasses. I wonder if anything I say will actually get written or if it'll all be censored before it's even published. I shouldn't have even bothered coming; I could have let Aiden do the interview on my behalf and saved myself the journey.

'The truth is,' I say, 'that I didn't have a clue what I was going to say until I opened my mouth on *Bold Women,* I hadn't planned it at all.'

'Oh. Don't you feel bad that people are paying a lot of money for a book that's basically a lie?'

'Not really,' I say flatly. 'Maybe I feel a bit bad about the people who bought it before I came clean when they thought it was real but now they know it's a lie they've only themselves to blame.'

Susie gives a cold smile.

'Don't you think you should offer them all a refund?'

'No.'

The waiter interrupts us by placing a steaming plate of spaghetti Bolognese in front of Susie. He flip flops around the table and places a bowl of creamy looking gloop in front of me with a hunk of bread in a basket.

'Mmm...smells delish.' Susie dives straight in and twirls her fork in the middle of the plate, twisting spaghetti and mince onto it in a great big clump.

I look at my hunk of bread and tap it - rock hard – if I attempt to eat that I'll have no teeth left.

'So,' she says through a mouthful, 'You think it's okay to mislead the public with a fictional diet that you've actually never even tried?'

There's a touch of dislike in her tone; so much for people liking honesty.

'Of course it's not okay to mislead the public but I'm not doing anything that the rest of the diet market isn't doing. I've never tried *The Travis Way* but I've been on pretty much every diet known to mankind and *The Travis Way* definitely *would* work if you stuck to it long enough and didn't die of boredom in the process. It's no different from all the other diet books - they all work if you can stick to them long enough. All I'm saying is that the people who tout the new wonder diet every summer and Christmas as being easy and requiring no effort are lying. To lose a shed load of weight in a short time you have to starve yourself. End of.'

'Hmm.' She studies her forkful of Bolognese. 'So exactly what point were you trying to make on *Bold Women*?

I think about this for a moment while she continues to ram Bolognese into her mouth and the smell of chicken soup drifts up to my nostrils.

'That all diets are the same, I suppose. They all have a gimmick but they're basically the same and all they really do is make you obsessed with eating.

For instance, I've been on so many diets that I could tell you how many calories are in that meal and pretty much any food you care to mention. I could probably tell you how many calories are in a lump of shit if I really thought about it.'

Susie looks shocked and I'm a bit surprised myself; I'm not too sure where that came from.

Susie stuffs another forkful of spaghetti into her mouth.

'So, really,' she says through a mouthful of food as she chomps it around her mouth; obviously no one has ever told her it's rude to eat with your mouth open. 'You're saying that the diet industry is one big lie?'

'I suppose I am. It's a million-pound business and fat sells but actually, I think diets make you fat. Every time I started a diet I'd lose weight for a few weeks and then fall off the diet wagon and put it all back on plus even more.'

She nods in agreement as I stare at her mouth; a mixture of brown mush and bloody worms tumbling around in a hideous washing machine.

My stomach does a lazy roll as I watch her fork dive into her plate for more.

I clamp my hand over my mouth and run.

* * *

I'm home at last and lying under a blanket on the sofa. When Seamus picked me up I made no attempt to answer his questions but simply closed my eyes and laid my head back on the headrest and prayed he'd get home before I threw up again. He didn't like it very much and made a few barbed comments about *people being ignorant* but I ignored him. He's definitely getting above himself and I think I'll be asking for a different driver next time.

The restaurant toilet was tiny to say the least – there's no way I could have even got inside it in my fat days. It wasn't overly clean either; I had to shut my eyes when I was throwing up down the toilet because just looking at the toilet rim was making the retching even worse. It was horrific and whoever professed to clean it should be thoroughly ashamed of themselves.

When I finally emerged after fifteen minutes, I was pale and shaking and felt as if I was dying. Susie looked mightily relieved to see me; her huge owl-like eyes blinked at me as if she couldn't quite believe what she was seeing; perhaps she thought I *had* died in there.

I don't feel so sick now but I can't bear even to think about food; even the memory of Susie eating is enough to set my stomach churning. I did manage to finish the interview – fortunately by the time I'd returned she'd finished eating and the plate had been taken away so I didn't have to watch her masticating. The soup and bread had gone too, thankfully.

Susie then went on to ask some very searching

questions about exactly how I lost all the weight and seemed very interested in the binging aspect of it. I have an idea that she now thinks I'm bulimic because I spent so long in the toilet. I tried to convince her that I'm not but I'm not sure she believed me – which just shows what she knows about it because I hadn't even eaten anything *to* purge. Anyway, who knows if she'll publish what I said but I find that I don't really care; I'm on a countdown to get these media things out of the way before I can go back to my old, quiet life.

I know what's really wrong with me, of course, what's really making me feel so rough.

Blake.

So. Our meeting.

Okay, I didn't attempt the Heimlich manoeuvre on him because actually, I don't think he deserved any help after his attempt to blackmail me. But of course I didn't stand and watch him die because I'm not a complete monster, I do have some morals.

No.

I walked away and whatever happened, happened.

I think he's probably alright because I'm *almost* sure that I heard the sound of footsteps coming up the stairs before I made my escape. I walked swiftly back through the doorway into the car park and then calmly crossed over to the other set of lifts and stairs. Once I'd reached them, I ran down the stairs that exit onto the back of the high street and then walked quickly back to where my car was parked, got in and drove home.

I'm sure if Blake *had* died it would have been on the local news or in the local paper because there's not a lot that happens in Frogham so it would definitely have made the front page. I've checked and rechecked all of the available news sources on the internet and there's absolutely nothing on there about a man choking to death.

I'm sure he's fine.

I would ring him to check but that's not possible because he doesn't have a phone anymore because I have it. Or did have it; the phone is now no more, as they say. I didn't care for putting my hand in his pocket to get it out because who knows what might have been in there, but needs must. Fortunately it was in the first pocket that I tried and I put my hand straight on it and nothing else – and he did grab hold of my wrist quite firmly once I had the phone in my hand but I managed to prise his fingers off without too much effort – he was choking, after all.

I had a brief moment of panic when I realised that his phone was password protected but luckily it was 1,2,3,4 so that didn't pose a problem. Maybe he ought to think about having a better password when he gets himself a new phone. I discovered that he only had one incriminating picture of me but I deleted all of the photographs on his phone just to make sure and then I went into his iCloud and deleted all of the ones in there too.

I took the precaution of taking the sim card out and stamping on it a few times and then I wrapped it in tissue and flushed it down the toilet. The actual phone also got stamped on and shoved inside a plastic bag and then I deposited it in the dog poo bin at the end of the street. I don't think anyone will be rooting through there looking for hidden treasure, do you?

I'm not totally heartless; I do feel a little bit guilty about what happened but it wasn't as if I made him choke, was it? Okay, I pushed him but only to stop him taking my money – if he hadn't lunged at me it would never have happened. It's his own fault really and to be honest, I wouldn't care if he did choke and die as long as I wasn't there and wasn't involved in any way. Annoyingly, because I happened to be there, I feel *slightly* responsible.

Which I'm sure is why I'm feeling so ill – which proves that I'm not totally bad and do have a bit of a conscience.

So I'm going to have to make sure that he's still alive or else I'm going to keep churning it over in my mind and make myself even more ill. I think I'll be safe from him blackmailing me now because I'm pretty sure that he won't have saved the photograph anywhere else. If by some remote chance he has then I'll say he must have Photo shopped it or something – people do it all of the time and you can never tell what's real and what isn't. I don't know why I didn't think of this before – mostly likely it was sheer panic - because I could have saved myself a thousand pounds and a lot of grief.

Never mind, too late now. What I need to do now is check that he's alive so that I can put it all behind me. I don't know where he lives - he could well be sofa surfing for all I know – but I *do* know that he works for an estate agent. I'm not sure if it's the same one that I bought my apartment from – I think he mentioned changing jobs when we were together but I wasn't really listening. There aren't that many estate agents in Frogham so it shouldn't be too much of a major task to ring them all.

What if I find out he's dead?

No point in worrying about it until I know for sure.

I pick my mobile up and punch in the number for Shipley's. A woman with a nasal voice answers and I ask for Blake Weaver. There's a pause before she informs me that no one of that name works there so I immediately hang up without continuing the conversation. A quick Google confirms that there are only three more estate agents in Frogham and I ring the biggest one next: Brothertons. They seem to take an awfully long time to answer and I ponder at how ironic it would be if Blake does work there because that's where Bella works.

Eventually the phone is picked up and I recognise Blake's voice instantly. I quickly press the end call button and heave a huge sigh of relief; he's alive so I can stop worrying that I might be implicated in his death. Although it wouldn't be murder, would it? Because it's not as if I'd tried to poison him or anything, is it?

I lie back on the sofa and feel the tension leave my body. I can stop fretting about it now so perhaps I'll start to feel better. I make a solemn promise to myself to try and be a better person – which I think is easily do-able provided no one tries to blackmail me again. I close my eyes and am just drifting off when my mobile rings; I pick it up to see *withheld number*. Could it be Blake? Of course not, I tell myself, he's not clever enough to remember my number and I took his phone so there's no way he can contact me.

It could be anyone of a million people trying to sell me something. I take a deep breath and press the button to answer.

'Hello.'

'Hello doll. You want to be a bit cleverer next time and withhold your number.'

Of course; my number must have flashed up when I rang the estate agents, what an idiot. I could kick myself for making such a rookie mistake.

'Nothing to say, doll?'

'Not really.'

'You left me to fucking die *and* you took my phone,' he hisses.

'Well, you're clearly not dead.' I answer calmly.

'No thanks to you.'

He's talking very quietly but he sounds mad,

really mad.

'I could hear people coming up the stairs so I knew you'd be okay.'

'Fucking liar. I don't know how you can live with yourself.'

'What do you want?' I cut in, having no intention of listening to his self-pitying drivel.

'I want my phone back and I want my money. I kept to my side of the deal.'

'No, you didn't. Anyway, I've disposed of your phone and I'm not giving you any more money.'

'I've got more photos. I'll go to the papers.'

'You haven't got any more,' I say with a snort. 'And even if you had I'd say they were fakes because you have no proof at all that we were ever together. You should be grateful that I gave you anything at all - now get lost before I make a complaint to your boss.'

Blake is silent and I almost expect to hear the whirr of his brain as he processes what I've just said.

'There's something wrong with you,' he says quietly, knowing when he's beaten. 'You're not right in the head.' And with that he hangs up.

I think he might be right.

CHAPTER THIRTEEN

Doris and I are watching the Tellytalk team as they set up their equipment. The team consists of only two people which was a bit of a shock as I was expecting a crew similar to the studio ones so was distinctly underwhelmed when only Jeff and Stefan turned up. Their equipment consists of a camera on a tripod in the window recess of my lounge and a huge spotlight placed to one side of it. They're going to film us for a screen test; we have to chat about a television show to see if we're going to be suitable Tellytalkers.

Some of the celebrities don't even film the show in their own home but go into the studio to film it – apparently some of the *Tellytalkers* don't like their own homes being shown on television because it feels like an intrusion of privacy so they use a mock-up instead. I don't really care; they won't be showing the outside of my apartment so no one is going to know where it is, and I wasn't offered the option to go into the studio anyway.

I'm obviously not famous enough.

The camera is a bit underwhelming – it's very small and looks just like one you could buy from Argos. Jeff has fixed it to a collapsible tripod that doesn't look particularly sturdy. The bright spotlight pointing directly at the sofa is already heating the room up and he's only just turned it on. I think we're going to be sweating buckets by the time we're finished. Neither of them is exactly talkative and Stefan, the producer, has hardly uttered a word, except to mutter *hello.* He's had his mobile phone clamped firmly to his ear and has been having whispered conversations since the moment he arrived.

Gerald was agog when I told him that I'd agreed to do the show but I explained to him that Aiden was insistent that I had to do either *Tellytalk* or *We're Watching You* to get the media off my back and that *Tellytalk* seemed the lesser of two evils. Gerald didn't say an awful lot but I don't think he's very impressed because it won't look too good in front of his posh friends but that's just too bad and there's nothing I can do about it. Although he did agree that it's preferable to going into *the mansion* because who knows what would happen then?

When Stefan contacted Aiden to arrange the screen test they suggested that I get a *Tellytalk* partner of my own choosing rather than let them pair me up with someone I don't know. They think it looks more natural if you already know one another. As Doris is my only friend I've asked her and to say she's over the moon would be an understatement – she nearly went into orbit when I asked her. She said she'd do it for nothing because she loves *Tellytalk* but Aiden has arranged for the production company to pay her – but not as much as they're paying me because obviously I'm the star. When I asked her if she wanted to do it she kept screaming *you're shitting me* and when she eventually calmed down she said it was her most favourite of favourite programmes.

After *We're Watching You,* of course.

I'm feeling better than I did and I'm sure I must finally be getting over this awful bug although I'm not fully recovered and not back to my normal self, I do feel heaps better. I slept quite well and I haven't felt sick at all today so I definitely think that now the Blake thing is sorted I'm on the mend. Luckily Gerald is working away in London for a couple of days so I haven't had to endure his constant nagging about seeing a doctor. By the time he comes back I'm hoping to be completely over this bug and back to my old self.

When Doris arrived and I opened the door to her she looked shocked when she saw me – I haven't seen her for a week and she thought I looked *like shit,* as she put it. She insisted on doing a full hair and make-up job on me which I was quite pleased about because I just didn't have the energy to do it myself; this awful fatigue is the aftermath of the bug, I assume. I now look *reasonably* okay, although my hair still looks dull and lifeless despite Doris's robust attempts with the hot brush. She pulled my hair so hard I expected to see most of it attached to the brush by the time she eventually gave it up as a bad job. I don't think it's going to matter too much because the spotlight is so bright that we're going to look bleached out anyway and now I come to think about it most of the *Tellytalkers* look slightly vampire-like on screen so they obviously get the arc light in the face treatment as well.

Before Jeff and Stefan got here Doris and I decided on our game plan. Luckily we're fans of the show so we know pretty much what's expected of us, although Stefan is apparently going to brief us when he eventually gets off his mobile phone. The first thing we had to decide on was Doris's accent – does she keep her fake, posh presenting, accent or be herself?

I said I thought that she should do what she felt most comfortable with – either would be fine. In the end she plumped for being herself because it wouldn't be much fun if she had to put on her phoney accent every time she opened her mouth. When she does *The Travis Way* road show it's all scripted and she pretty much knows it off by heart but she said when she has to think on her feet, or backside, as we'll be sitting down, it's much harder to keep it up.

We then debated what to wear – some of the *Tellytalkers* are dressed up to the nines; full face of slap including false eyelashes, glamorous designer outfit which they blatantly name drop about, towering stiletto heels, hair extensions, the full works. Then there are others who go the complete opposite way; joggers and sweatshirts with unkempt hair and a *just got out of bed and haven't even brushed my teeth yet* look, and there's one couple who wear pyjamas and slippers. Doris and I had to decide which camp we were going to be in and after a lot of thinking about it we decided on neither. We would cut straight down the middle and go for smart casual; jeans and semi-smart tops with cute fluffy socks on our feet so that it doesn't look as if we're trying too hard.

'So.' Stefan reluctantly tucks his mobile phone in his trouser pocket. 'We're nearly ready. Just need to run through a few things before we start.' He gives his shaggy beard a good scratch before continuing and I wonder what might be lurking underneath that unattractive, pubic hair-like beard.

'Firstly, be yourself and don't try and put an act on.'

I look at Doris and raise my eyebrows and she winks; she's made the right choice and the *Tellytalk* viewers will be getting the real, unadulterated Doris and not Doris light.

'Secondly, don't worry about swearing or not being PC because we'll edit anything not acceptable before it gets to air.'

He's not being truthful because they don't edit *all* of the bad bits. From what I've seen of the other *Tellytalkers* anything goes; there's a lot of bleeping of swear words because some of the *Tellytalkers* are unbelievably foul mouthed and every other word is a swear word. The public don't seem bothered and I think some of them swear even more than they normally would for the shock effect. I don't believe the not being PC thing because even if they bleep it you can still lip read what they're saying. They still deliberately leave in the most controversial stuff to get the viewers to keep watching and don't care how bad it makes the *Tellytalkers* appear. The production company can pretend to be PC whilst letting the viewers see exactly what's being said because it makes for more shocking telly. An old couple on the show were practically hounded out of their home for a mistimed joke; they took their salt of the earth observations a bit too far when watching an episode of a celebrity *Mr and Mr.* The old feller made a quip about thinking that LGTB was a type of sandwich and the remark went global; Twitter went into absolute meltdown over it and they were absolutely destroyed. What had previously been praised as a down to earth no nonsense attitude was turned into rampant homophobia and they were oofed off the show quicker than you can say *perpetually offended.*

So Doris and I will have to be very careful – Stefan might say they can edit it but I don't think they will if it makes for good ratings. I'm not homophobic or racist but a remark made in the wrong place and we could be done for. Doris and I have agreed to give each other a sly kick on the ankle if we think either of us is over stepping the mark but I'm starting to wonder whether agreeing to *Tellytalkers* was the right decision.

'What we'll do is put the programme on and you can watch it through on your own to give you a chance to think what you're going to say about it and then we'll run it through again and start filming. You okay with that?' Stefan couldn't sound more disinterested if he tried and I can see his hand twitching towards his mobile phone in his pocket.

'Yes,' Doris and I say in unison.

Stefan pulls his phone out of his pocket.

'You got good internet speed?'

'Of course,' I say, although I actually have no idea.

'Good. I'll push this episode onto your TV and we'll get started.' He picks the remote up and turns the television on.

'Password?'

'Four zeros,' I say reluctantly.

I watch as Stefan punches the buttons.

'What we watching?' Doris asks.

Stefan doesn't answer but taps his phone and the screen comes to life with the opening credits for *Doctors Appointment.*

Great. A programme about people with

unsavoury medical conditions who are too embarrassed to see their own GP but don't mind sharing it with millions of people on national television; complete with close ups and graphic descriptions.

'Ooh, I love this,' Doris says.

'Really?' I watched it once and that was more than enough.

'Yeah. I fink I missed my vacation. I love anyfink medical. I should have been a nurse.'

'You? A nurse?' I try not to laugh.

'Yeah.' She looks offended. 'Why not?'

'No reason, I'm just surprised that's all. I'm sure you'd make a great nurse.'

Doris looks slightly happier when I say this and I think I've fooled her but I'm not being horrible – alright maybe I am – but don't you need a degree to be a nurse? With the best will in the world I can't see Doris studying at university for three years. Or even three weeks actually. She can't tell the difference between a vacation and a vocation so I think she'd struggle. Although I could be doing her a massive disservice because I never thought she could transform herself into *Doe* and to look at her on stage you'd never believe she was the same person.

'Yeah, I always fancied the uniform,' she goes on in a wistful manner, 'Either that or a firewoman, I wouldn't mind doing that neither.'

I flatly refuse to feel bad now; there's about as much chance of Doris being a nurse or a firewoman as there is of me telling the truth for the rest of my life.

We watch the TV and are introduced to this weeks extremely young-looking doctors who all seem far too nice and perky for my liking. The first patient is wheeled out, a miserable looking, seventy-two-year-old with a badly fitting toupee who wants some Viagra because he's just got married to someone a quarter of his age.

'Do you fink they're real people?' Doris asks thoughtfully.

'Sadly, I do.'

'I dunno how they can do it, show themselves up on telly like that. You should see the fings people go on there with, it's unbelievable. One bloke went on there cos he fought he smelled 'cos people kept sniffing around him and when the doctor examined him it turned out he wasn't wiping his arse properly.'

I don't say anything because what *can* I say? That's the level of the programme we're supposed to make interesting and witty conversation about.

The newly-wed is eventually sent on his way with a smile and a prescription for Viagra clutched in his hand after answering some cringe inducing questions about him and his bride's sexual habits; there's also been quite a bit of chit chat about the weather and the state of the world and it all seems very jolly. All very unhurried and as if they have all the time in the world; not like real life where you have barely five minutes to state your ailment and get out so the next patient can come in to repeat the process.

The next patient appears on screen; six-feet-four in his stocking feet and built like an armoured tank. He drops down heavily into the chair, nearly flattening it in the process and I'm sure I can hear the legs creak. After several minutes of pointless small talk about the weather and the state of the world (again) the doctor asks how he can help. Rubbing his hand across several days growth of black stubble, the patient quietly tells the doctor that he's wants a sex change and is aiming to start transitioning by living and dressing as a woman as soon as he can afford to buy some clothes. He'd like the doctor to put him forward for surgery and thinks that a boob job and hormone tablets would be a good start.

'Fuck me,' Doris says in amazement. 'Why is it the trannies are always built like brick shithouses?'

I give Doris a sly kick on the ankle.

Thank God this is only an audition and not the real thing.

* * *

By seven o'clock it's all over; Jeff packs his camera and huge spotlight away and Stefan shoves his many pencils and pads of paper that he's made no attempt to write on, into his duffle bag – all whilst clutching his mobile phone which appears now be welded to his hand. He then shrugs himself into his biker jacket – although he came in a van – and both he and Jeff are out of the door and gone with barely a *goodbye*. No opinion was given as to whether they thought we were any good as *Tellytalkers* and as they were leaving Stefan muttered that they would review the footage and get back to me.

Part of me hopes that they'll decide we're rubbish and they don't want us but the realistic side hopes that they *will* want us because otherwise I'll have to go in *the mansion* and take my chances there. Being famous is no fun, I can tell you.

I shut the front door on them and go back into the lounge to see Doris returning from the kitchen with two wine glasses. She sits down on the sofa and picks up the bottle of prosecco that she's bought with her.

'Dunno about you but I could do wiv a drink. Didn't know talking could be such hard work and those two weren't no laugh a minute neiver.'

I flop onto the sofa. 'You're right, even though we've only been watching telly it's hard going when someone's watching you and you're trying to say the right thing.'

'I didn't bovver after a while, couldn't be arsed. If they don't like me, tough shit.'

This is true; I gave up on kicking Doris after the third time because she took absolutely no notice of me and simply moved her feet.

'Anyway,' she goes on, 'I didn't fink much of them neiver, especially that beardy weirdy Stefan. Looked like a proper paedo.'

'How can he look like a paedo?'

'Dunno, he just did. Gave me the creeps.' She shudders.

She expertly eases the cork out of the bottle and then pours us both such a generous glass of prosecco that it practically empties the bottle.

'Cheers!' We chink glasses.

I take a sip of mine and realise straight away that I don't want it. It tastes vile.

'You alright Al?'

'I'm fine.' I put the glass down on the table; it's no good I can't drink it.

'Don't you want it?'

'Maybe later. Should probably eat something first, we've had nothing since breakfast.'

'I could go out and get somefing or we could order in a Chinese or somefing.'

My stomach rolls at the thought of greasy chicken and mushrooms floating in a watery sauce. Not again, for God's sake.

'You still got that bug fing?'

I nod. 'Had it all week. I think it's on its way out now but I still feel a bit dodgy, it's definitely hanging around.'

Doris glugs her wine and narrows her eyes at me over the top of the glass.

'Maybe you ought to go to the docs, get yourself checked out. Make sure it's nuffin serious, a bug shouldn't last that long.'

'I'm alright, apart from feeling really tired, I'll be back to normal in a couple of days. Anyway you sound just like Gerald, he's been non-stop nagging me about the doctors as well. No wonder no one can get an appointment if everyone goes every time they get a bug or a virus. It's not like the telly where the doctors have all the time in the world to waste.'

''Gerald only nags 'cos he loves you.'

I smile and debate telling her about the engagement and decide not to. Not very much longer until we'll be going ring shopping and then we can go public properly and I can show off my engagement ring. I think I might go for a sapphire instead of a diamond, be a bit different. A big one, obviously.

'You ain't denying that he loves you.'

'He's a very good friend,' I say primly.

Doris snorts. 'Friends? Give over, it stands out a mile that you're shagging.'

'Does it?' I can't help laughing.

'Course it does, I guessed weeks ago. I'm pleased for you Al, you deserve someone nice to look after you.'

I feel suddenly choked; she wouldn't say that if she knew what I was really like.

'What's the matter? You look like you're gonna cry.'

'Of course I'm not.' I *never* cry, not real crying anyway although I do a very good fake cry. 'I'm just feeling under the weather, that's all.' What the hell is wrong with me? 'Here.' I push my glass of prosecco along the coffee table next to hers. 'I'll only waste it so you might as well have it, I don't really fancy it.'

Doris stares at the glass and then looks at me and bursts out laughing.

'What? What's so funny?'

'It's fucking obvious, innit?'

'What's obvious?'

'You're pregnant.'

'What?' I look at her in shock. 'Of course I'm not. Why would you possibly think that I'm pregnant?'

'Frowing up?' She raises an eyebrow.

'I've had a bug and anyway I've been sick *all* of the time, not just in the morning.'

'That's an old wives tale about being sick in the morning, it can happen anytime of the day.'

'Can it? You seem to know a lot about it.'

She looks a bit uncomfortable. 'Only what me mum told me; she fought she had a bug when she was up the duff with me. She couldn't keep nuffin down and was puking for months. She was on the pill and she still got preggers.'

I'm not even on the pill but surely it's not possible; Gerald and I haven't been *shagging,* as Doris puts it, for very long at all.

'I can assure you that I'm most definitely *not* pregnant.'

'Sure about that? When was your last period?'

I think about this; my periods have never been

what you'd call regular, even when I was fat. Once I lost the weight they became even more sporadic and in the last year they've pretty much vanished altogether.

What if I am pregnant – what would Gerald have to say about that? We've only been together for a few weeks so how would he feel if I hit him with an unplanned pregnancy before we've even managed to get engaged? Knowing him he probably wouldn't mind but I would; I have absolutely no desire to have a baby at this point in my life. Or ever, actually, although I suppose I'll have to at some unspecified time in the future as I'm sure Gerald will want children.

'Well?'

'Well what?'

'When was your last period?'

'A couple of weeks ago,' I lie.

Doris looks disappointed.

'Oh. You sure?'

'Of course I am.' I laugh. 'So bang goes your theory.'

Doris wanted to go out and get us a McDonalds but I told her that I still felt rough and I didn't think I could face any food just at the moment. I told her she should get herself something on her way home; not very subtle, was I? And she did take the hint because she drained her glass of prosecco and left with a *I hope you're feeling better soon*, she didn't even bother to drink my wine so she must be annoyed with me. Although she'd have been over the limit if she had so I've done her a favour in a roundabout way.

As soon as I'd closed the door on her I got my phone out and Googled *morning sickness* to see if it was at all possible that I could be pregnant. I didn't like what I found; that typically morning sickness can start between four and sixteen weeks of pregnancy. I counted back to when Gerald and I first got together and realised that it *was* nearly four weeks ago. I also factored in that I'm not on the pill and didn't use any contraception at all because I'd sort of assumed that as I'm not having periods I couldn't get pregnant. Dr Google tells me this is not the case at all as I could very well get pregnant without having periods because I might be *about* to have a period and then *not* have one because I'm pregnant. All very confusing but the upshot of it is, I could, in theory, be pregnant.

These facts were enough to propel me out into the car and all the way to the out of town Tesco's – luckily open all night – where I purchased a pregnancy test. Well, two actually, because conveniently there are two in a pack so I can be doubly sure of the result. I paid for them at the self-service desk before checking that no one was watching me.

And I'm now sitting in the bathroom trying to force myself to pee on the stick and get it over with. Could I be pregnant? The more I think about it the more possible it seems. I need to find out because if I am pregnant I have absolutely no intention of having a brat and the sooner I find out the easier it'll be to have a termination. I did some more internet searching and discovered that at under ten weeks all that's required are a couple of pills and bob's your uncle, back to normal. I have plenty of money and could go private so I wouldn't have to be doing any of that NHS queuing nonsense. And while I'm about it I'll get myself some contraceptive pills to make sure it doesn't happen again. In fact I need to do that, pregnant or not.

I can't be more than four weeks pregnant so it won't a problem time wise for taking the abortion pill and what Gerald doesn't know about won't hurt him. I have a sneaking suspicion that he'd be pleased and think it was meant to be if I told him because he's a bit soppy like that so it's on a need to know basis – no one but me needs to know.

I know all this but I'm still dithering around and I just need to get on with it so I can sort it out and get myself un-pregnant if the worst has happened. If I am pregnant I have Doris to thank for suggesting it because it had never even crossed my mind. Imagine if I hadn't realised until it was too late for a simple termination? It doesn't bear thinking about.

Okay; time to bite the bullet.

I pull the stick out of the packet and read the instructions.

Here goes.

CHAPTER FOURTEEN

I used both of the tests, just to be sure.

And there's no doubt about it, they both say *pregnant.*

After I discovered this I thought that I'd be tossing and turning all night but I slept amazingly well, considering, and for the first time in over a week I've eaten breakfast this morning and managed to keep it down. I think I'm not fretting about it because it'll be easily sorted and I'm just grateful that I've found out now before it's too late.

Although I do find it thoroughly annoying that I've spent nearly two weeks throwing up and not being able to stand the sight of food and I've barely eaten and I haven't lost any weight at all, not an ounce, which is most unfair. When I got on the scales I expected to see that I'd dropped a few pounds at least but incredibly I've stayed exactly the same. I don't know how this is possible but there it is; it's no doubt due to all of the hormones whizzing around my body so the sooner I get rid of them, the better. I also feel a bit bloated around my waist although this is most likely my imagination because I'm hardly going to be expanding at four weeks; or it could be water retention, I suppose.

After a bit more research with my trusty friend, Mr Google, I've found a private clinic forty miles away in Reading - not in Frogham, because knowing my luck someone who knows me or more to the point, knows Gerald, will spot me going in there and broadcast it to the entire world. Reading is a large enough place for me to be anonymous but close enough to Frogham to be able to get home quickly and easily after I've taken the pills. Or pill. It seems that I take one pill at the clinic and then another at home the next day. From what I've read on my internet searching it's pretty straightforward and will only require me to make one visit as I'm barely pregnant at all.

As soon as it's nine o'clock I'll ring them and fingers crossed, I'll get an appointment for today. I think I will, because money doesn't just talk it *demands*. I'm feeling quite calm about it all and I'll be forever grateful to Doris for suggesting it because otherwise it would never have crossed my mind. I wouldn't have realised until I'd started putting weight on and by then it would involve a lot more than taking a couple of pills.

I've decided to treat Doris to a nice present when

Gerald and I go ring shopping to London at the weekend; a big thank you for being a life saver - even though she doesn't know it.

Because I certainly won't ever be telling her.

* * *

Honestly, I should be a secret agent.

I've parked in the massive multi storey in Reading so if by some remote chance someone recognises me I have my cover story ready. I'll say that I'm clothes shopping, which isn't a complete lie because depending how I feel I might well have a browse. According to the map on my phone the abortion clinic is only a ten-minute walk away from the car park and even if the pills work really quickly – which I'm sure they won't, I think I can manage a ten-minute walk back to the car. The clump of cells is only about the size of a coffee bean so I can't see it'll be that bad - although I'll have to lie to Gerald about it and tell him that I'm having a heavy period, which I will be in a way, so it isn't really lying.

The clinic blurb does suggest that if you're apprehensive about having an abortion you can bring a friend or relative along for moral support – although they're not allowed into the consultation. For the briefest moment I considered asking Doris but quickly dismissed the idea. I'm not apprehensive but some company would have been nice but unfortunately I just don't trust anyone enough to confide in them, which I blame Mother for because she was the most suspicious person in the world and it's obviously rubbed off on me.

I get out of the car and look at my watch; in my haste to get here I'm way too early and have an hour to kill before my appointment. Retail therapy first, then, instead of afterwards.

I chuckle to myself as I stride across the car park to the exit; an hour to kill – rather apt really.

* * *

I bought myself a very nice dress from Reiss, a tad expensive but I felt in need of a treat. It's a knee skimming, floaty little number in pale cream and I know Gerald will love it on me, although I don't think I'll be wearing it this weekend in case I bleed on it. I also bought Doris a lovely silver Pandora bracelet which will look lovely on her dainty wrist. Although I'll have to think of a reason to give it to her because I can't exactly tell her the truth. I could say it's for all her hard work on *The Travis Way*, I suppose, she'll never guess the real reason because I think I was pretty convincing yesterday.

I carry the bag containing the dress and the bracelet back to the car and put it in the boot because I don't think I should take it with me. Although the clinic clearly states that they don't judge you for your decision to terminate a pregnancy, I don't want to arrive with the evidence of a shopping trip in my hands and appear to be cavalier about the decision I've made.

The thing is I don't feel pregnant at all and barely four weeks doesn't really count as being pregnant does it? Because quite often you can have a late period which is actually a minor miscarriage - and you wouldn't even know it was a minor miscarriage, you'd just think you were late. I've learned an awful lot from my internet searching and I feel very well informed now so I can make sure that I'm never caught out again.

I close the boot and re-check the route on my phone; it's straight out of the car park and all the way along the main shopping street and then turn right into a smaller side street. I set off and decide to take the stairs rather than the lift; what if I took the lift and it broke down and I got stuck there all day? Irrational I know but I just want this over and done with as quickly as possible without any hiccups. I semi run down the three flights of stairs and emerge from the grubby stairwell into the watery sunshine. Shoulders back, I set off and march along at a steady lick and marvel at how much better I feel; even my hair doesn't feel quite so lank and lifeless today – there's the merest hint of a bit of body in it for the first time in weeks.

I'm quite surprised by the outside of the clinic when I finally manage to find it, I've actually walked past the door twice and had to retrace my steps to find it nestled between a chemist and an old-fashioned bookshop. The street numbers ran in a most confusing way; ending with odd numbers on one side of the road and then continuing with both odd and even and I had to double back on myself several times and start counting again before I spotted it. It's fortunate that I allowed myself plenty of time to get here.

The entrance is a very non-descript black door with *WBS Ltd* on a small plaque next to it and a well-worn button to press on a shiny brass intercom.

I press the button and wait.

While I'm waiting I watch as an elderly man in the bookshop shuffles around carefully arranging books in the window, brushing the dust off the ones that are already there with a mangy looking feather duster. I'd be surprised if he ever sells anything at all as the books look as if they've been in the window for years and the book jackets are faded from the sun.

He looks up from his dusting and smiles at me and I smile back. I wonder if he knows that right next door to him women are having unwanted pregnancies flushed away like used toilet paper. I shake the thought away and wonder where the hell that thought came from; it must be the pregnancy hormones because didn't I nearly cry yesterday when Doris was nice to me? I did, I can't deny it; so that's another very good reason to get rid and get back to normal before I turn into a quivering, emotional wreck.

Although if motherhood makes you soft why didn't it work on Mother? I never saw her cry; not once, although I don't recall her ever laughing much either, except at me.

A tinny voice from the intercom interrupts my thoughts; it asks my name and once I've replied I'm buzzed in. I climb the very narrow and steep stairs and am confronted by yet another door. I push it open and emerge into a bright modern reception which is in stark contrast to the ancient stairwell.

'Alison?'

The receptionist beams up at me from her desk and I confirm my name. She's no sooner ticked me off a list than the door to the left of her opens and a nurse wearing a blue uniform appears.

'Hello Alison, I'm Theresa. If you'd like to come with me?' She smiles at me kindly and I smile hesitantly back. It all feels a bit too pleasant – as if I'm here to have my hair cut and blow dried rather than dispose of an unwanted pregnancy.

I follow nurse Theresa into a small room with two comfortable looking chairs arranged around a small table holding a vase of flowers and a box of tissues. There's a large window along the back wall which is covered by closed venetian blinds and the room is lit by a flickering strip light which I suspect could bring on a fit if you were in here long enough. Theresa sits down and I sit in the chair opposite her and look at the tissues and wonder if I'm supposed to cry. I decided I'm not going to; I don't need to prove anything here.

'Now.' She picks up a clipboard and pen. 'A few questions and then we'll get you sorted.' She smiles again so I smile back.

We run through my details and I give her my doctor's details and consent to inform him of my decision to terminate my pregnancy. I consider refusing permission in case someone there knows Doris or Gerald but then stop myself – I'm being paranoid and ridiculous and patient notes are confidential for God's sake.

'Okay, what was the date of your last period?'

I've given this question a lot of consideration and I've decided that I'm going to lie and say my last period was five weeks ago. I know there's no actual reason to lie but I thought it would be simpler than having to explain *the not had a period for ages thing.* I want this over and done with as quickly as possible and not have to sit here yakking about it. It's not a complete lie anyway because if I'd had a period it could well have been five weeks ago.

'Five weeks ago,' I say.

'Okay. That's fine, although we do double check with a scan just to be sure of your dates.' She scribbles on the clipboard. 'That would make you well under the limit for the mifepristone and misoprostol.'

I look at her blankly.

'The abortion pill.'

'Oh, I see.' I can't think how I missed that in my

internet searching or maybe I didn't miss it and have just forgotten. Is it possible to get *baby brain* this early? I've read that being pregnant can affect your memory and thinking and make you feel a bit fuddled but surely not this early? Most likely I've had so much going on – the Blake thing, the interviews – that my brain is overloaded and I've been ill too, so that could be why.

'Alison?' Theresa is looking at me with a quizzical expression and I realise that I've been lost in my thoughts of a load of old rubbish; really, I seriously need to get a grip.

'Sorry,' I say, 'Miles away.'

'It's understandable.' She smiles again. 'Now, are you completely sure that this is what you want to do? We do have counsellors available to talk it through with you if you're unsure about your options and you're very early on in your pregnancy so you have plenty of time. You don't need to make a decision today.'

'No, I'm quite sure. It's not the right time in my life to have a baby.'

She looks at me and smiles and I think she's waiting for more of an explanation. I smile back and we sit in uncomfortable silence for a full minute.

'Okay,' she says, as she finally realises that I have nothing further to add. 'It's totally your decision. Did the contraception method you were using fail or did you not use any?'

'I didn't use any.'

She frowns.

'Was there any particular reason you didn't use any?'

'No, I just forgot,' I say lamely.

'I see. It might be best to look into contraception options to make sure that you're protected for the future. We can arrange an appointment with a birth control advisor for you and you can discuss it with her – there are the obvious methods such as the pill and condoms but we also offer the contraceptive injection and also the implants. The injection covers you for thirteen weeks and the implant can protect you for three years. If you ask Anna on Reception she can arrange an appointment for you.'

I nod. She obviously thinks I'm useless and need to have the implant otherwise I'll be back here in a couple of months with another unwanted pregnancy.

'Now, there are some facts that you need to be aware of. If you do decide to go ahead you will bleed after the abortion and it will normally continue lightly for one to three weeks afterwards, but times can vary. Your normal menstrual periods will usually return after about four to six weeks. The heaviest bleeding typically occurs two to five hours after using misoprostol and usually slows down within twenty-four hours. Do you have any questions?'

I shake my head and congratulate myself on bringing a towel to sit on in the car on the way home.

'I do have to tell you about the risks involved although they are minimal and I'll also give you information to take away with you in case you're unsure. You can, of course, call us at any time if you're worried.'

She then proceeds to tell me in great length all of the possible side effects that could occur and what to do in the event that they do. I stifle a yawn and wish we could dispense with all of the talking and just get on with it.

'Now if you wish to proceed with the abortion you have to read and sign this consent form – although even once you've signed it you can of course change your mind at any time before taking the medication.' She hands me the clipboard and pen and I pretend to read it carefully but I don't, I really can't be bothered. After what I think is a suitable amount of time I scribble my signature on the form and hand it back to her.

'I'll take you back out to Anna where you can pay and then we'll take you through and get your scan and blood pressure done.'

Of course.

Nothing happens until I've paid.

* * *

Anna has relieved me of nearly seven hundred pounds after assuring me that the transaction will show on my bank statement as Dresden Ltd, which is the company that owns WBS Ltd and will give no indication that I've attended an abortion clinic as they also perform cosmetic surgery. I hadn't even thought of this and can't say I'm particularly bothered because no one sees my bank statements except me.

I'm now lying on a hard metal table with my stomach exposed waiting for a different nurse to do an ultrasound scan on me. I've had my blood pressure taken, which was absolutely fine, and I'm eager to get this done so I can have the pills and be on my way. Theresa has told me that as I'm young, fit and under six weeks pregnant I can take the second pill at home if I wish to instead of coming back - which suits me just fine because it seems ludicrous to drive forty miles to swallow one little tablet.

The nurse doing the ultrasound is brisk and after introducing herself as Fenella, she studies the screen and then launches straight to the job in hand and with a quick *this is going to feel cold I'm afraid* she plops ice cold gel onto my stomach. The coldness makes me jump and I flinch.

'Sorry,' she says, not sounding sorry at all.

She places the scanner over the gel and begins to move it, spreading the gel out over my stomach as it moves. The scanner looks very much like the self-service *scan and go* hand held scanners that they have in Foodco but without the security tag on. I almost want to grab it off her and have a go myself.

I can't see what's on the screen because it's turned away from me so that only Fenella can see it – apparently women who are having an abortion don't like to see the scan but I wasn't bothered either way. It's not as if it's even going to look like a baby, it's going to be an unrecognisable blob so I'm hardly going to get weepy over it.

She rubs the scanner over my stomach with her left hand whilst keeping her eyes on the screen and using her right hand to move the mouse around and tap the odd key on the keyboard.

'You say your last period was five weeks ago?' she asks while studying the screen.

'Yes,' I lie.

She continues scrutinising the screen and clicks the mouse a few more times and then repeats the scanning process of slowly sweeping it down to near my pubic bone and upwards and across several times, pressing quite hard as she goes. After a few minutes of this she removes the scanner from my stomach and carefully wipes it with a cleaning wipe and then hands me a wad of tissues. She doesn't seem as friendly as Theresa and Anna and the room is silent while I wipe the gel off and get up off the bed and put my skirt back on. I feel slightly uncomfortable and as if I should make conversation with her but cannot think of a single thing to say. I'm just about to give in and make an inane comment about the weather to relieve the silence when she gives the mouse a final click and stands up.

'If you come with me, Theresa will be with you shortly.'

I get up and follow her back through to the room that I sat in with Theresa and once I'm through the door Fenella shuts it smartly behind me and leaves me there. I settle down on my allotted seat and wait. Ten minutes go by and I wonder what's taking so long; if they'll just give me the pills I'll be on my way. In fact now I come to think about it why can't I just take both the pills with me and take the first tablet when I get home instead of taking it here? It'll save any possibility of ruining the upholstery on my car seats with blood seepage.

Yes, I think I'll suggest that because she's only going to watch me swallow it which seems pretty pointless to me.

'Sorry to keep you waiting.'

'No problem,' I lie.

Theresa sits down opposite me and studies her clipboard.

'O-k-a-y, we seem to have a bit of a problem.'

'A problem?'

'Yes. It appears that you're *not* five weeks pregnant.'

I *knew* it. I'm not pregnant at all - just my luck to get two duff pregnancy tests. I thought they were a bit on the cheap side. I should have gone for the branded ones but my reasoning was that two cheap ones were going to be exactly the same as the branded ones but in a different package. Maybe

I should have bought four to be completely sure, but honestly, what are the chances of getting two tests that are both duff? Pretty small, I'd say. Not that it matters now. I should write and complain to the manufacturer because it's really not good enough.

I had my suspicions when Fenella was performing the scan – she did it twice, which now makes perfect sense because she obviously couldn't find any sign of a pregnancy at all. What a waste of time. I wonder if they'll give me all of my money back or charge me for the scan and the consultation? They can't charge me for the pills because I won't be needing them. I decide I'll make a fuss if they don't give me *all* of my money back because really, they should do a routine test when you arrive just to make sure that you really *are* pregnant. I'm relieved that I'm not pregnant but I don't think that's any reason to let them off the hook too easily.

I stand up ready to leave.

'Where are you going?' Theresa gives me a strange look.

'Well if I'm not pregnant there's no point in staying is there?'

'Please sit down, Alison.'

'Why?' I demand.

'Because you *are* pregnant.'

'What?' I sit back down. 'You're not making sense. You just said I wasn't.' I can hear the annoyance in my voice and no doubt Theresa can too.

'No, I said you weren't *five* weeks pregnant; I didn't say you weren't pregnant.'

'I'm sorry, you've lost me.'

'According to the scan you're fourteen weeks pregnant.'

I stare at her in shock.

'But that's not possible.'

'I'm afraid the scan doesn't lie. You are most definitely fourteen weeks pregnant. Fenella took head measurements and they clearly show that your pregnancy is of fourteen weeks gestation.'

'But...' I stare at her uncomprehendingly.

'The period that you thought you had was actually breakthrough bleeding. It's quite common and in most cases nothing to worry about. The foetus appears perfectly normal on the scan if you do decide to proceed with the pregnancy.'

I gawp at her, unable to speak.

'It's a shock.' She smiles sympathetically.

'I can't be fourteen weeks pregnant,' I say again before the awful truth hits me with the force of a speeding bus.

Blake.

CHAPTER FIFTEEN

I'm barely answering her but Doris hasn't even noticed because she's so excited about Tellytalk. According to Aiden, Stefan and the production team were super excited with our screen tests and were delighted to offer us both a contract for six shows. All I can say is that Stefan kept his super excitement very well hidden. Maybe it was underneath his beard.

I didn't sleep at all last night and have been wandering around from kitchen to lounge all morning going over the events of yesterday and I only stopped my aimless wandering when I was interrupted by Aiden, ringing to give me the news about *Tellytalk*. And then the very minute that I'd finished speaking to him Doris rang me and started blathering on and on and hasn't drawn breath for what seems like forever.

I have a sneaking suspicion that Aiden rang Doris before ringing me because how could she have rung me so quickly otherwise? More proof of his infatuation with her and his contempt for me. Not that I care; I have other things on my mind.

Unable to concentrate on Doris's gabbling any longer I decide that I've had enough; I just want to not speak to anyone while I try to work out what I'm going to do.

I briefly consider just hanging up on her but then decide not to as she'll most likely assume we got cut off and ring me straight back.

'Sorry, Doris,' I cut in, mid flow. 'I have to go now, there's someone at the door.'

'Oh. Alright.' I can tell she doesn't believe me but I hang up anyway.

I need to concentrate on two problems. Firstly, Gerald and I are supposed to be going engagement ring shopping at the weekend and I have to think of a suitable excuse as to why I can't go. Nurse Theresa refused to give me the abortion pills yesterday because I'm past the legal limit to take them so I'm still pregnant. I now have to have a surgical abortion, so there's absolutely no way I'm going to be feeling like tramping around shops looking for an engagement ring. I asked if they could do it there and then but she said no; a doctor has to perform the procedure and the earliest they can fit me in is tomorrow. She was a bit vague on the details and couldn't say for sure whether I'd be given a sedative to make me sleepy or a general anaesthetic to knock me out completely; apparently the doctor will make that decision with me when I see him, or her, tomorrow.

She also said that I need to take someone with me as I won't be able to drive home and that someone will need to stay with me at home for twenty-four hours afterwards to make sure that I don't have any complications. I did consider lying and pretending that someone was waiting outside for me and then driving home myself but quickly dispensed with that idea. Most likely they won't do it if I don't take someone in with me and I don't want to take the chance and have to delay it until the following week.

There is only one person that I can possibly ask and that person is Doris; which means I'll have to confide in her about the pregnancy so maybe I shouldn't have just cut her off mid-sentence and pissed her off.

I won't tell her the whole truth because I'm definitely *not* going to tell her about Blake. I'll make up a phantom one night stand because I won't be able to bear the look of pity and disgust that will be written all over her face when she realises that I'm one of the *saddos* that dropped their knickers for him. The situation is bad enough without having to contend with that as well.

I took a good, long look at myself in the mirror this morning before I got dressed and without a doubt I have the beginnings of a bump and my stomach definitely feels harder and rounder. I just wish they could have done the abortion yesterday so it was over and done with because I can't say I'm looking forward to it at all; taking a couple of pills is all very well but surgery? No, I can't say I fancy that at all; not helped by the fact that last night I made the monumentally stupid mistake of Googling *surgical abortion* and was very nearly sick. I just hope they decide to knock me out completely because I don't want to be awake and aware of anything that's going on. I think as I'm paying, I'll have to insist.

I'm going to have to ask Doris about tomorrow right now because I really can't leave it any longer and I don't know why I didn't ask her just now instead of lying so I could get off the phone. Not thinking straight; or more like not thinking at all. Perhaps she can help me come up with an excuse to get out of seeing Gerald at the weekend. And tonight too; because he's supposed to be coming round for the evening and I don't have the energy to face him.

I flump onto the sofa and turn the television on. I can't stand the silence or the thoughts that keep tumbling around in my head; even watching ancient re-runs of *Antiques in the Attic* where people trundle out their hideous old tat is preferable to the memory of Mother telling me that one day I'll get what I deserve and that it'll serve me right.

* * *

I'm waiting for Doris to arrive; I didn't ring her but texted instead:

Please can you come round asap but don't tell anyone

Suitably mysterious enough to pique her appetite and get her round and also I just didn't have the energy to ring her. I'd have had to explain myself to her and it's better to do it here than over the phone – what if one of her many family members happened to be listening in on the conversation? It'd be all around Frogham before you could utter *treetops telephone*. Anyway, she's obviously forgiven me for hanging up on her because she replied instantly with *on my way*. She's a good friend but I'm under no illusion that she'll also be gagging to find out what's going on.

In less than fifteen minutes the doorbell rings and she arrives. I wonder if she's somehow guessed that I'm pregnant? She seemed very knowledgeable about pregnancy the other day and maybe I wasn't as convincing as I thought. I answer the door to let her in and she steps into the hallway and wraps her arms around me.

'Mate, what's the matter? I could tell somefing was up on the phone.'

I find a peculiar kind of comfort in her arms as we stand there and the dratted hormones make me want to cry again but I successfully fight it.

I step back out of her arms and walk into the lounge. 'Come on in and I'll tell you.'

We sit on the sofa and I can't think what to say.

'What's up, mate?'

'I've got a bit of a problem.' Understatement of the year.

'Yeah?'

'I'm pregnant.'

'I fuckin' knew it!' she shouts.

'Yeah, you were right,' I say ruefully.

'I fought you said you had a period?'

'Apparently it was breakthrough bleeding,' I lie.

'What?' She's totally confused and I realise that I'm going to have to tell her the whole story. Or bits of it.

'The thing is, Doris, when you asked if I was pregnant I thought it wouldn't hurt to check because it wasn't much of a period that I had and I started to wonder if maybe you were right. I always keep a couple of pregnancy tests in the bathroom just in case so I did one and I got a bit of a shock when it came out positive.' More lies.

'Ooh, I bet.'

'I decided not to tell Gerald because we've only been together a short while so I thought I'd just get the abortion pill and that would be that.'

'Yeah?'

'Anyway, long story short. I can't have the abortion pill because I'm fourteen weeks pregnant. I have to have an operation.'

The room is very quiet and the silence hangs as I wait for Doris to say something.

'I fought you said you and Gerald have only been

together for a few weeks?'

'We have,' I admit.

I watch as realisation dawns on Doris's face.

'Oh Shit.'

'Exactly.'

'So.' Doris frowns, 'If it ain't Gerald's, whose is it?'

* * *

I told Doris that I had a one-night stand with a man called Lars who I met on *Tinder.* She said she never even knew that I was on *Tinder* and I said well of course I wasn't anymore and he was the only person I met off there and he'd put me right off. I didn't exactly say that he'd raped me or anything but I did let her think that maybe I got talked into doing something that I didn't really want to do and that he plied me with a lot of alcohol. I said he'd told me that he came from Sweden and was frequently in London on business - because that way I could keep it suitably vague and not have to make up lots of lies about him that I'd then have to remember.

I told her that after our first date he hadn't bothered contacting me again – which I was relieved about – and I hadn't contacted him and I'd deleted my account on *Tinder*. I thought I did quite well with the cover story, all things considered.

I think she was quite pleased that I'd confided in

her and she promised that she wouldn't tell a soul. She also came up with the perfect excuse for not seeing Gerald tonight or at the weekend – I should tell him that she was pregnant and I was helping *her* out by going to the clinic with her and looking after *her* over the weekend. And he had to promise me that he wouldn't tell anyone because Doris hadn't even told her mother.

Quite brilliant, I thought. I must admit I was very impressed and Doris has gone up a notch in my estimation. I know that Gerald won't blab to anyone about Doris because he's a man of his word.

Unlike me.

I do feel uncomfortable lying to him; he really deserves a much better fiancé than me. Once this is all over I've promised myself that I'm going to try really hard to be a better person because I don't *have* to be like Mother and I don't *want* to be.

I rang Gerald while Doris popped home to get an overnight bag; she's going to stay here tonight as we have quite an early start and tomorrow night too as I need someone with me for twenty-four hours after the operation. Gerald was so sweet when I spoke to him and believed what I was telling him *totally*. He was really concerned for Doris and angry that she'd been left in the lurch by a man; he said I was such a good friend to her and that of course it wasn't a problem – we could go shopping next weekend. I started to feel quite emotional because he was being so nice so I told him Doris was back and I had to go.

She is back now and I have to admit to feeling a bit relieved; I wasn't relishing the thought of what's going to happen tomorrow and knowing that she's going to be with me is making it a bit more bearable.

These pregnancy hormones are making me soft.

* * *

It feels quite different going to the clinic with someone else rather than going on my own. I'll be glad to get today over with and then I really *will* turn over a new leaf. As we were getting in the car I remembered that the dress and the bracelet that I bought for Doris were still in the boot but I left them there. It wouldn't feel right giving Doris the bracelet today, I'm going to wait until this is all over and give it to her then. I have something else for her too, something that reminds me of Mother that will be very useful to Doris because I don't want it anymore. Mother and I are done and I want no reminders of her in my life.

We park in the multi storey car park again and begin our walk to the clinic. Unlike the fine weather of Tuesday, today it's lashing down with rain and as we hurry through the streets under our umbrellas, I wish the hours away until it's all over. Doris has guessed I'm nervous and told me not worry, she says she's sure they'll give me a general anaesthetic because otherwise they wouldn't have told me not to eat or drink anything this morning. She says they'll give me an injection and it'll be as if I've closed my eyes and opened them again and it'll all be over. I've never had a general anaesthetic so have no idea but Doris has – she had her tonsils out when she was fifteen - and she says it brilliant, like taking drugs, only legal.

I hope she's right.

Once we're buzzed in and I give my name to Anna, the smiling receptionist, who I think remembers me anyway, Doris and I settle down in the only two seats in the tiny waiting room. I contemplate the logistics of an abortion clinic; there's apparently no stigma attached anymore but I don't think anyone broadcasts the fact that they're having one do they? Does the clinic manage the appointments so that they never overlap thus ensuring that you never see who's before or after you? I think maybe they do or it could just be that it's a slow day in abortion land.

Before we sat down I gave the receptionist my debit card so she could take the additional payment straight away because as soon as it's done I want to leave; I don't want to be hanging around here a moment longer than necessary. I didn't even look at the amount when I put my pin number in, I couldn't seem to focus properly. She did say something about crediting me with the cost of the pills from Tuesday but honestly, I don't care.

I feel as if I have *butterflies in my stomach*; fluttering movements as if a whole flock of them are trapped in there, whirling around. I've heard the expression used many times but never actually felt it before. All due to the lack of food and lack of sleep, no doubt.

And the fact that I'm terrified.

'Alright, Al?'

'Yeah, fine,' I lie, stretching a semblance of a smile across my face. 'Just got butterflies, you know.'

'Butterflies?'

'Yeah, you know, nervous tummy, butterflies flapping around inside.'

Doris stares at me with something like horror.

'What?'

'Nuffink,' she says. She looks down at the floor to avoiding looking at me.

'Tell me.'

'Na, it's nuffink, honest.'

Being an accomplished liar myself I can spot someone lying from a mile away and I put my hand on her arm. I have no idea what she's lying about but I find that I suddenly *have* to know.

'You can tell me,' I say with a fake smile. 'I'm a big girl.'

'It's nuffink.' She shrugs and I continue to stare at her, holding her gaze while I wait for her to reply. She finally relents and sighs.

'It's just somefink me mum used to say.'

'What's that?'

'Well, you know I told you she didn't know she was up the duff?'

'Yes.' Get on with it for God's sake.

'She said that she should have known sooner 'cos she felt me moving and she weren't even free months pregnant. She fought it was wind 'cos it felt like somefing flying around inside her.'

I stare at her.

'Miss Travis?'

Theresa's voice interrupts us from the doorway to the treatment rooms.

'Would you like to come through? Your friend can wait here for you.'

I stand up and walk towards her, vaguely aware of Doris telling me she'll see me soon.

I just need to get this over with.

* * *

It's very quiet in the car on the way home and it seems very strange to me that Doris is driving and I'm sitting in the passenger seat, it's the wrong way around because it's my car and *I* should be driving.

Thankfully it had stopped raining by the time we left the clinic to begin our walk back to the car although the sky was so black with rain clouds that it felt much later than four o'clock. I was grateful for the gloom because I couldn't stand the thought of it being a lovely day – although I don't recall why I thought that. As we passed the bookshop I think I remember looking in the window and seeing the elderly man arranging the books again but now I'm not so sure; was it today or was that on my first visit? More importantly, why does it even matter?

Every so often Doris asks me in a concerned voice if I'm okay and I reply that *I'm fine* and to prevent her from keep asking I do my trick of putting my head back on the headrest and closing my eyes. It'll be easier on both of us that way - she doesn't know what to say and I'm hardly making it any easier for her.

I thought I could get today over with and I'd be back to normal in no time but that's not going to happen; I'm not the person that I thought I was. I'm not Mother who would have had an abortion at the drop of a hat and continued her day as if nothing at all important had happened. I'm sure if *she'd* been aware that she was pregnant before it was too late, I'd have been sucked out and flushed away without a moments regret.

That's something to be thankful for at least; I'm *not* my mother.

'That's it Al, have a kip,' Doris says patting my leg with her child-like hand. 'Bet you're fucking knackered.'

I don't answer but I don't think one is required. I am knackered and I also have a bit of a headache which isn't surprising because I've eaten and drunk nothing all day. I was offered a cup of tea at the clinic before we left but I refused as I just wanted to get out of the place as soon as possible and get home.

I'm in a state of shock, I know that. Maybe it's just as well.

I'm still pretending to be asleep when we arrive in Frogham and I keep my eyes closed until we pull up outside my apartment building. Doris gently shakes my shoulder and I act as if I've just woken up. She's parked next to her own car and I don't bother to tell her that she should have parked in the underground garage because all I want to do is get inside and shut the door and go to bed. We climb out of the car and I watch as Doris presses the key to lock the doors.

'Nice car, Al.' She pats the bonnet as she walks around the car towards me. 'Shame it weren't a nice day cos we could have got the roof down.'

I don't say anything but trudge towards the entrance and Doris follows behind. She insists that we get into the lift instead of walking up two flights of stairs even though I tell her that *I'm fine*. We arrive outside my apartment and I rummage around in my bag to retrieve the key and then fumble trying to get it into the lock but my hands are shaking so badly from the lack of food that I can't seem to manage it. Doris gently takes the key out of my hand and unlocks the door and we go in.

I take my shoes off and place them neatly on the doormat and remove my coat and hang it on the coat stand. I then make straight for the sofa and sit down.

'Cup of tea, Al? Bet you're gagging.'

'Yes, please,' a small pathetic voice says. I think it was me.

I hear the distant sounds of the kettle being filled and cups and spoons being removed from cupboards and put on my lovely quartz worktop and I remember that I felt like this once before; when Mother died. I know that I'm in shock but I also know that it'll soon pass.

Doris appears with two steaming mugs of tea and a packet of biscuits under one arm. She places the cups on the coffee table and starts to open the biscuit packet.

'I don't remember buying any biscuits,' I say, as if it's important.

'You didn't.' Doris sits down next to me. 'I bought 'em wiv me 'cos you never have no food in your house.'

She offers me the packet and I take one; I need to eat something to try and get rid of this headache.

'When I've drunk me tea I fought I'd go and get us a takeaway or somefing.'

I take a sip of tea and bite into the biscuit, a chocolate digestive. I didn't want it but as the chocolate hits my tongue I'm suddenly ravenous and I greedily wolf it down and reach for another.

'So what do you fancy – Chinese, Thai or do you want fish and chips? The chip shop down Ipswich Street does a lovely cod and chips or a pie if you don't like fish.'

'Cod and chips.' I decide.

'Yeah, fink I'll have that too.' She looks at her

watch. 'I'll go now and then we can settle down wiv the telly for the night and not 'ave to go out again.'

'Oh, I'd forgotten you were staying the night again.'

'Course I am, I ain't gonna leave you on your own, am I? You have to have someone wiv you for twenty-four hours to look after you, remember? I wouldn't be much of a friend if I just fucked off 'ome, would I?' She drains her coffee and stands up.

'Honestly, Doris, you don't need to stay, I'm fine.

'No, you're not. No way am I going and I ain't having no arguments about it.'

I look at Doris, my only friend, and tears spring to my eyes as the stupid hormonal emotions threaten to swamp me yet again.

'Really, I'm fine.'

Doris opens her mouth to argue and I realise that I'm not making myself clear.

'Sorry.' I put my hand up to stop her talking. 'What I meant to say was that I'm still pregnant.'

She stares at me open mouthed.

'I changed my mind. I didn't through with it.'

CHAPTER SIXTEEN

'You didn't go frew wiv it?'

'Nope.'

'But you were in there for ages.'

I was.

I'd signed the redrafted consent form, had my blood pressure taken and listened while Theresa talked me through the procedure and all of the possible side effects and what I should expect afterwards. It had seemed to go on forever and I'd just wanted to get it over with and not have to think about it anymore.

She'd then left me alone to remove all of my clothes and put on a voluminous, blue cotton gown with a flapping open back and for some unknown reason, a pair of long white, over the knee socks. I sat and waited and eventually she came back and collected me and I followed her along a narrow corridor to another room with a narrow, high bed that was more like a trolley than a bed. I had a very bright lamp on a tripod over one end of it which reminded of the one that Jeff bought for the *Tellytalk* screen test.

I tried not to look too closely around the room at the long white counter and various stainless steel trays with covers over them because I think I was starting to panic then about what and how they were going to do it.

Even though I already knew exactly what was going to happen because I'd read it on the internet and once you know, you can't un-know, however much you might want to.

Theresa helped me climb up onto the long, narrow bed and I had to lie down flat. She then produced a white waffle blanket and pulled it over me right up to my neck as if I were a child and she was tucking me in for the night. At least, that's how I imagine a child would be tucked in, because Mother's bedtime routine was to turn out the light, slam the door and leave me alone in the dark.

Then we waited in silence for the doctor to arrive.

Just one scratch, I kept telling myself, because that's what Theresa had told me. One little scratch and I'd close my eyes and when I opened them again it would all be over and I'd be back to normal and no longer pregnant and it would be as if none of it had ever happened. Well, apart from the bleeding, but I could just pretend to myself that it was a heavy period – lie to myself – because I'm extremely good at that.

I fully intended going ahead with it too, I tell Doris as I fill her in on the details, because I did. I had absolutely no intention of having a baby and definitely not with Blake as the father (I didn't tell Doris that bit, obviously) but when it came to the crunch, I just couldn't.

It was the flutterings that decided it, I think, although the doubt was there already and I think I would have backed out anyway. When I thought I was four weeks pregnant and I searched on the internet for abortion information I felt quite okay about taking the abortion pill, because in my mind it would be nothing more than a late period.

But fourteen weeks?

I'd seen the pictures and it no longer resembled a clump of cells, it looked like a *baby*. I've never had strong opinions or been anti abortion and I'm not anti abortion even now, but this was *me* that it was happening to and no one else and all of the sensible reasoning about it *not being the right time* and *being unplanned* didn't apply.

It was raw emotion and there was no fighting it.

Theresa was very kind considering that I'd left it until the very last minute to change my mind. The doctor had come in and introduced himself and asked me if I had any questions and I'd said *no* and everything was proceeding as it should until the moment he took hold of my hand to administer the anaesthetic. Theresa placed her hand lightly on my shoulder – I assume they do that to everyone to reassure them - and I thought, *this is it, it'll soon be over*, and then I opened my mouth and told them to *stop* and that I'd changed my mind.

'Fuckin' 'ell, Al.' Doris stares at me, round eyed.

I laugh, because otherwise I might cry.

'They were okay about it,' I say. 'Wasn't a problem at all. I don't suppose I was the first and I'm sure I won't be the last.'

They didn't seem surprised but I suppose they're trained not to show any reaction. They didn't ask me if I was sure but helped me to sit up and I swung my legs over the side of the bed and sat there while they scribbled a few things on clipboards and in cardboard files and generally faffed about. Reflecting on it now I think they were just giving me some time to think things through and to be sure of what I wanted. After five minutes of this Theresa did say that if I changed my mind again in the next few days to let her know but I shook my head and said no, I wouldn't be coming back.

Theresa took me back to the other room and left me there to get dressed. After what seemed like ages she came back to collect me and wished me well and said she hoped things worked out for me. She told me to see my own doctor as soon as possible to sort out my maternity care and that really brought it home to me then – what I'd done.

I'm going to be a mother.

But I did the right thing, I'm sure of that.

The only thing.

'So there it is, Doris. I'm going to have a baby.'

'Fuck.'

We both laugh and I feel the tension of the past few days start to dissipate.

'You ain't 'alf brave, Al. Wish I was like you.'

I shake my head. 'No, I'm definitely not brave, Doris.'

'Well I fink you are.'

I'm about to tell her how frightened I am by it all but stop myself; why spoil her illusions? She's going to be the only person who will think anything good about me for a long, long time so I'd better make the most of it.

'So. That's that.' I say. 'Now are you going to go and get those fish and chips or are we going to starve to death?'

She laughs.

'The fing is though Al, wot are you gonna do about Gerald?'

Ah yes.

There is that.

* * *

At seven o'clock on Saturday morning I get a text from Aiden informing me that he's sent me an email and that I *must* read it immediately.

Does that man never sleep? Does he have any sort of life at all? I'm sure he's not human and that when he's not out getting free meals from his clients he's hanging up in a wardrobe somewhere like a bat.

I open up the email to see that he's been contacted by *Woman Today* to say that they're running my interview with them this week; attached to the email is an advance copy that I'm to look at and if I'm not happy with it I'm to let them know before Monday morning.

Sounds to me as if I'm definitely not going to like it if they'd had to send it to me in advance. I close the email without opening the attachment. I really can't be bothered to look; I have more important things to think about such as being pregnant with another man's child whilst being engaged to someone else.

Gerald.

I have to tell him; I may be an accomplished liar but I don't think even I could convince him that I'm four months pregnant with his baby when we've been together for barely four weeks.

He texted me last night to ask if Doris was okay, and if *I* was okay. I texted back saying that she was fine and so was I.

So I didn't actually lie.

Such a nice man; far too nice for me – not that he's going to be so nice when I tell him the truth. I'm actually doing him a favour because he deserves someone much better than me although as I've said before, I am trying to improve.

If I'm going to have this baby – and I most

definitely am – then I'm not going to be a copy of Mother.

History is *not* repeating itself; I won't be locking my child in the cellar or slapping it for crying or telling it that it's a useless lump every minute of the day.

I'm not going to be completely honest with Gerald – I'm trying to give up lying but Rome wasn't built in a day and it's not that I'm doing it for totally selfish reasons. I'm not going to tell Gerald about Blake; I've decided to keep it simple and stick to the story about the *Tinder* date which doesn't actually show me in a very good light either - but at least it won't look as if I'd been seeing someone else for months when I wouldn't let Gerald near me. I think that would be just another kick in the groin for him and he really doesn't deserve it.

It's all such a pity really because I could have had a very nice life with Gerald. I really took to Bunty and Jeremy, they're absolute diamonds and I think that they rather liked me too. It's a shame, but there it is.

Perhaps in another life.

There's nothing I can do about that but at least they'll be there for Gerald, he won't be having to cope alone like I always have because he'll have Bunty and Jeremy to support him. If I could avoid hurting Gerald I would but it's just not possible and I will genuinely miss him, despite his *going on*.

As Mother was fond of saying, you've made

your bed and now you've got to lie in it and she'd probably also say that I'm no better than I should be.

Which I'm not; but a lot of it is her fault.

I'm going to text Gerald and ask him to come round here so I can break the news to him. I briefly considered meeting him for dinner in a restaurant and telling him the bad news there, thus avoiding any outright nastiness as there would be other people about and Gerald wouldn't want to make a spectacle of himself in public.

The coward's way out, obviously.

But no, I'm not going to do that, even though I am a coward. No, he can come here and shout at me and call me all the horrible names that he wants to because actually, I thoroughly deserve it, and it's a very small price to pay for the way I've treated him. He can get it all off his chest and hopefully that might make him feel a bit better about things and be some small compensation. And then he can go away and find someone much nicer and more suitable, someone naturally thin, too, because he has no shortage of admirers and can take his pick.

Once I've got that out of the way I need to make some plans of my own. Firstly I have to make an appointment at the doctors so I can get my antenatal care and maternity plan sorted. I've already got a pretty good idea of what I require – plenty of pain relief and hand me the baby when it's all over, thank you very much. One of those epidurals that I've read about sounds just the ticket and if they could pop it in the minute the contractions start that would be even better.

Fortunately I don't have to worry about money at all – even before *The Travis Way* started selling I had enough money to last me for a long, long time and now I have even more so I don't need to get a job or anything tedious like that.

I *could* afford a nanny if I wanted one but I think I'll have a bash myself first and see how it goes – I mean, how hard can it be? Mother managed it; she might not have made a very good job of it but I survived, didn't I?

I quite like the idea of being a stay at home mum and going out for walks and stuff. Doris has offered to pitch in and help and says she's an expert with babies because she has lots of nephews and nieces from her two brothers. I had a quick browse on the internet last night and got quite excited looking at all of the baby kit that you can buy and some of the baby outfits are just adorable. I'm quite looking forward to kitting out the nursery; it'll give me something to do while I'm waiting. I think I might wait until I get to the six months stage though; don't want to tempt fate.

My phone pings and a message from Doris pops up complete with a hearts and flowers gif:

Hope ur ok! Thank you so much! You're the best! I can't believe how much that birds worth! Xxx

She's obviously found the note I put in her bag last night about the bird. When she went out for the fish and chips last night I asked her to get the shopping bag out of my boot and bring it back with her. When we'd finished eating I gave her the bracelet and she was so thrilled. She put it on straight away and said she was going to wear it all of the time. She did ask why I'd bought her a present and I told her that I'd been meaning to get her something for a long time because she'd been such a good friend to me and helped me get over the death of Mother and everything. She said I didn't need to give her a present but I could tell she was thrilled.

When I came back from taking the empty plates out to the kitchen, I took the ugly bird down from the bookcase and when I sat down I gave it to her. She looked a bit puzzled and I told her that I was giving it to her to sell so she could use the money to spend on something she wanted. This really confused her so I explained that it used to belong to my grandparents but Mother had always hated it so it seemed wrong for me to keep it, somehow, and I'd be much happier without it. I said she should look on it as a bonus for all of her hard work for making *The Travis Way* such a success.

She turned it around in her hands and said *fanks very much* but I could see she didn't get it; she obviously thought it was a bit of old tat suitable for the dustbin and of absolutely no value at all. I could tell by her face that she thought the hormones were affecting my brain and I'd gone a bit mental; perhaps I have.

I'd decided to get rid of that bird and the only reason it was still here was because I've had other things on my mind. I'd started to feel uncomfortable with that ugly thing peering down on me because every day it reminded me more and more of Mother; ugly and twisted, and I felt as if she was watching me. Stupid, I know, because she's dead, but I felt her presence; perhaps it's the hormones again but I'm taking no chances, it had to go. It was only saved from the rubbish tip by a stroke of fate. Whilst I was pacing the lounge and agonising over my predicament and watching re-runs of *Antiques in the Attic*, I saw a bird just like it. The absolute double of it; a middle aged man from Worthing had bought one from a car boot sale for a pound (so not strictly an antique in the attic) and taken it along to the show to get it valued. Repulsive and hideous it certainly is, but incredibly it's also extremely rare and sought after and worth the best part of thirty thousand pounds; a nice amount for a deposit on a house or whatever Doris decides to spend it on.

I wanted to make sure that she didn't throw it out or leave it on a bus or something so I put a note in her handbag with the link to the website that has one for sale just like it - and from her message I'd say she's just found the note.

I text back *you're welcome xx* and then toss my phone down on the duvet. It's way too early to ring Gerald to ask him to come over – I'm going to ruin his day but there's no need to do it at seven o'clock in the morning. Let him have a lie in before I break the bad news.

There's also Blake to consider; I will have to tell him that he's going to be a father but not just yet. I'm sure he won't be in the slightest bit interested and will run a mile but I have to give him the opportunity to be involved because I'm not Mother.

I'm *not* like her.

Most likely he'll be horrified and knowing how his brain works he'll think that I want money off him; I don't want anything from him at all but he has to *know*, because it's his child too. There's also the very good chance that he'll find out for himself anyway as I'm going to be on *Tellytalk* and I have a bump that is only going to get bigger and once it's in the media there'll be no hiding it.

Honestly; I hope he does run a mile because I'd rather he wasn't involved at all but I feel I have to do the right thing. Also, it's the opposite of what Mother would do and that can only be good.

Although it would be a lot more straightforward if he'd choked to death because I could then truthfully say that my child's father is dead, but that's the way the cookie crumbles, I suppose. I'm *not* wishing him dead; I'm just saying it would have made things a lot easier if he was.

I pick my phone up again and click on the email from Aiden; there's no possibility of going back to sleep now so I might as well read the article and get it over with.

Not that I care, they can write what they like.

I read through it quickly and then reread it more slowly. From what I remember of the interview – in between the feeling nauseous and throwing up in the toilet – Susie has pretty much quoted me word for word. The only difference that I can see is the asterisks in place of the letters when I said that I could probably tell her how many calories are in a lump of shit, or s**t as she's written. She's also inserted comments of her own that she obviously didn't say at the time but thought of later, quite clever comments actually, but all in all, it's a true representation of the interview and flows quite nicely.

I don't know how people will respond to the article but it doesn't really matter because once the episodes of *Tellytalk* are out of the way I'll be disappearing back to obscurity and *The Travis Way* will be yesterday's news.

And I'll be a mother.

I look at my phone; it's still only half past seven so I think I'll have a shower and get dressed and then text Gerald.

Time to do the right thing.

CHAPTER SEVENTEEN

Five months later

This baby is going to be early when everyone who knows anything about childbirth has told me she's going to be late.

Two whole weeks early.

I have both of my bags packed and ready to go; one for me and one for the baby and they're neatly arranged by the front door ready to pick up and take with me. It seems surreal to think that when I return to my apartment from the hospital I won't be alone – I'll have my daughter with me. The nursery is all freshly painted and furnished with the very best of everything that money can buy, everything that a baby could ever need and probably a lot of stuff she'll never need.

I look at my watch – again – I only rang Doris five

minutes ago and I know she'll be here in less than ten but I wish she was here *now*.

When I got up this morning I thought I was having the Braxton Hicks contractions that I seem to have been having all the time for the last month. Usually once I've showered and dressed they calm down – or maybe I don't notice them so much, but today they haven't; they've got much stronger and are starting to feel uncomfortable and I'm pretty sure I'm in labour.

I look at my watch again, a whole two minutes have crawled by.

I have plenty of time to get to the hospital because I know that I'm going to be in labour for a long, long time because she's my first baby, and first labours always last forever. So I've been told.

I just want Doris to hurry up so I get to the hospital and get an epidural done before it starts to hurt. I'm a complete coward and the thought of being in pain brings me out into a cold sweat. I don't like this feeling of being out of control and that my body is calling the shots.

I've been assured by the midwives that an epidural won't be a problem because it's *my* choice, *my* birth plan and *I* get to decide how this baby is born.

Provided, of course, that there's a doctor available and they're not too busy to give me an epidural because I'm not a priority - in which case I won't get to decide what happens at all.

This is why I'm getting agitated; I'm frightened

that the power is going to be taken out of my hands and I won't have any choice about anything at all and I'll be at the mercy of everyone else.

I haul myself up from the sofa and waddle over to the window and peer down into the street looking for Doris's car. There's still no sign of her so I waddle back to the sofa and carefully lower myself down into it and then change my mind and heave myself back up and waddle back to the window again as if somehow this will make Doris appear.

I'm huge now and look as if someone has stuffed a gigantic inflated balloon up my dress and then pumped it up a bit more for good measure. My ankles are swollen to elephantine proportions; all due to water retention which will apparently disappear like magic once the baby has arrived.

When I used to be fat, my waddlings around Foodco were usually met with looks of pity or disgust. Now I get sympathetic smiles and perfect strangers ask me *when is it due* and people want to know whether I'm having a boy or a girl and one elderly gentleman even insisted on carrying my shopping bags to the car for me. So obviously some forms of fat are more acceptable than others.

Doris is going to be my birthing partner – she's been to the ante natal classes with me and even came on the visit to the maternity unit at the hospital which frankly, I could have done without. You can know too much and I would have got out of it if I could but my lying didn't work no matter how I tried; midwife's are impossible to argue with whilst managing to stay extremely polite and calm at the same time. I've informed Doris that she's to stay at the head end and not the business end because there are limits – although I am very grateful that she's going to be there because, honestly, if it were the other way around and Doris was having a baby, I don't think I could do it for her.

The other mums to be and their partners at the ante natal classes assumed that Doris and I were gay and that this was *our* baby. We didn't tell them otherwise because it's none of their business and we have no need to explain ourselves. We thought it funny that people make such assumptions when they know nothing about you -although I'm sure one or two of them must have seen us on *Tellytalk* so it could well be that the whole of the UK *Tellytalk* audience think that we're gay.

They want us to do another series. We filmed the six episodes very quickly, pretty much back to back over a week – well before it was obvious that I was pregnant and we both went down very well with the audience. Doris's off the cuff remarks proved a big hit and she is naturally very funny without even trying and the viewers just loved her. She even has a fan club on Facebook where they post her latest observations on life. According to the producers she's a perfect foil to my rather deadpan remarks and sarcastic humour and together we make a very good double act. Incredibly, of all of the current *Tellytalkers* we're the viewers' favourites - which I find very strange because I was totally being myself – for once. I made absolutely no attempt to be witty *or* entertaining and secretly hoped that I'd be consigned to the cutting room floor. Which just shows that there's no accounting for taste.

Although I haven't watched it myself. I couldn't bear to.

The Travis Way still sells but nowhere near the numbers that it was selling before. Aiden tells me that this is quite normal because diet books have a limited shelf life and with Christmas on the way cookery books are way more popular at the moment. We had to stop the road shows once I started to show because people don't want to buy diet books from a fat pregnant person.

Aiden's words, not mine.

He didn't hide his revulsion from me when he heard the news of my pregnancy – I'm assuming Gerald told him because I certainly didn't. Although he hasn't actually *said* anything nasty to me because I still earn him lots of money.

I could see it though, in the flared nostrils and downturned corners of his mouth; a look very similar to the one he had when he heard the story of Warren shitting himself on the breakfast television sofa. Which I'm absolutely fine about because I can't stand him either – although part of me wishes that if somehow I could arrange for him to spend half an hour in Mother's company it would be *awesome*, because he wouldn't last five minutes with her. This is what happens when you're pregnant, you see, your brain goes off on a tangent and you have these ridiculous daydreams about absolute nonsense and dead people.

I watch through the window as Doris's car careers around the corner and into the car park where she pulls up sharply right outside the door. She's still driving her battered Fiat because she used the money from the sale of the Mother bird to put a deposit on a little terraced house in George Street. She should get the keys by the end of the month and has big plans for a makeover; it's just around the corner from her mum and dad's which I think means her dad will be doing the decorating.

I go out to the hallway and open the front door in anticipation of Doris's arrival and then pick up a bag in each hand. I straighten up to see Doris standing there, she looks hot and flustered and must have run up the stairs at full pelt to get here so quickly.

'I'm ready,' I say, stating the obvious.

'Gimme them bags.' She says with a wheezing breath. She really needs to give up the cigarettes.

'I'm fine, they hardly weigh anything.'

She ignores me and takes them from me and I let her because it might calm her down and it's hardly worth arguing over.

'Is that everyfing?' she asks as I step into the hallway and pull the front door closed behind me.

'It is.'

We walk towards the lift and Doris swaps the bags to one hand and puts her other hand under my elbow to guide me along.

'What *are* you doing?'

'elping you.'

'I'm having a baby – I haven't suddenly lost the use of my legs or my brain.'

Doris sniggers and drops her hand.

'Just trying to help, Al.'

I smile a tight smile as the doors swish open and we step into the waiting lift.

I breathe in through my nostrils to try to calm myself as we descend to the ground floor and I think ahead to what's in store for me.

I just want it to be over with.

* * *

We drive out of the car park and onto the main road.

'Ave you told Gerald?'

'Nope.'

'Don't you fink you should?'

'No. I'll tell him when it's all over.'

Ah yes, Gerald, my ex fiancé.

Amazingly we're still friends – we weren't friends for quite a while after I'd told him about being pregnant but we are now - which is all down to him because as far as I was concerned, he'd definitely never speak to me again and who could blame him?

When I told him, at first he couldn't understand what I was talking about. He was stunned and I had to explain to him very carefully and slowly that I was pregnant with another man's child. He said he couldn't comprehend that I would behave that way – because he clearly doesn't know the real me. For a short while he seemed to think that what I was telling him was some hideously unfunny joke.

When the truth finally hit him it wasn't nice; he didn't explode with anger as I'd expected but broke down in tears. I've never seen a man cry before and it was truly horrible. I'd have much rather he shouted at me and called me a disgusting person because I totally deserved it. Then he dried his face and straightened his shoulders and left without another word. He was dignified once he'd got his emotions under control and I couldn't help but feel impressed with him and then I felt sad that I'd thrown it all away. I didn't see him again for over two months until he arrived unannounced at my door one sunny Saturday afternoon. Incredibly he still wanted us to be friends – he told me that he couldn't never see me again just because I'd make an awful mistake and that although, obviously, the engagement was off, he didn't see why we couldn't still be friends like we once were.

I'd missed him – a lot, surprisingly, and was only too pleased to renew our friendship and although it's not the same as it was before, and never can be, we've sort of got past it and are on good terms.

'He said he wanted to know when you went into hospital,' Doris prompts.

'I know,' I agree. 'But he's better off not knowing because I could well be in labour for days and he'll only fret.'

He will fret and the least I can do is spare him that.

'Okay, your choice.' Doris shrugs.

I've also told Blake about the baby; I'd promised myself that I wouldn't be like Mother so I had to tell him. I didn't want to meet up with him but I didn't have his mobile number either so it was a bit of a problem. Then, after a lot of thought I put my lying skills to good use and rang the estate agents where he worked and made up some cock and bull story about being a client and needing to contact him. I wasn't optimistic that it would work because I did wonder whether they'd give me his number but they did so immediately - so they're obviously desperate for business because they didn't even bother to check the fictional name that I gave them.

I texted him and asked how he was to make sure that I had the right number and he texted back immediately with *leave me alone doll.* I then bluntly typed that I was pregnant and he was going to be a father. I could see that he'd read it almost immediately – but he never replied.

That was over a month ago so fingers crossed I'll never see him again but I have a clear conscience because I feel that I've done my duty and told him.

'Nearly there, Al.' Doris glances at me as I squirm in the seat and try to get comfortable. The contractions seem to be getting stronger and closer together, if this is what early labour is like what the hell is it like in the later stages? So much for contractions being a bit *uncomfortable*, which is what the annoyingly upbeat antenatal class leader told us. Thank God I'm having an epidural.

'I'm sorry, Doris,' I say, as she executes a handbrake turn into the hospital car park.

Doris screeches to a halt, yanks the handbrake on and kills the ignition simultaneously.

'What you sorry for?'

'Well, either my waters have broken or I've just wet myself all over your seat.'

* * *

I knew something like this would happen; first labours last for hours and hours and progress very slowly and there is no need to rush to the hospital at the first twinge. Doris and I were informed of this many, many times in the ante natal classes because mums-to-be always arrive far too early and have to be sent home again. Several of my fellow class mates expressed their fears that they wouldn't get to the hospital in time and would have their babies alone and unattended at home and were met with barely concealed derision from the healthcare professionals, because that *never* happens.

Well it's happening right here, right now. I had to be helped and practically dragged from the car by Doris and a nurse. I was somehow stuffed into a wheelchair and then wheeled through reception and on into the maternity unit. I fully intended getting out of the car and walking in but when I tried to swing my legs round from the foot well to get out, I found that any movement was impossible because of the excruciating pain of a watermelon trying to forcefully exit my body from my bottom.

I was whisked straight past admissions and down to the delivery suite where the door was swiftly closed and I was helped to stand up from the wheelchair to get onto the bed.

I thought I was going to die and would have happily lain down on the floor to give birth rather than take the three steps to the bed but when I suggested this the midwife laughed and said I'd be *fine*. It wasn't *fine* and the pain was indescribable in that short journey but somehow I was manhandled onto the bed where Doris practically undressed me on her own and then pulled on a hospital gown over my head. I'm now lying on the bed with the back propped up and my huge belly has a belt strapped over it to monitor the contractions.

The only thing that is keeping me from screaming as loudly as possible is the thought of the epidural that will soon be administered, although I honestly don't think I can wait very much longer.

'When is the doctor coming?' I ask the midwife through gritted teeth. She's calmly reading through my notes and doesn't seem in the slightest bit concerned that I'm dying.

'The doctor?'

Another contraction hits and I squeeze Doris's hand to a pulp and grit my teeth as I ride the wave of pain. I hear Doris whimper and wonder if this time I've actually broken her fingers.

'For my epidural,' I manage to gasp as the pain subsides to a more manageable level.

She puts down my file and comes over to the bed and studies the monitor and then pats my shoulder.

Helen Trasker, I read on her name badge, as she stands there, *Senior Sister.* I'm sure she told me that on my arrival but I had other things on my mind.

'An epidural? Oh no, it's far too late for that I'm afraid.'

I stare at her in horror as another contraction hits and this time I do scream; long and loud.

'Yes, won't be long now,' Helen confirms.

* * *

Helen is weighing the baby and will then give her to me to hold. I'm so exhausted that I'd be quite happy to have a sleep first and hold her later but I have the feeling that it wouldn't go down very well if I say that.

Doris cried when the baby was born – I have to keep calling her *the baby* because I haven't decided on a name yet – but I didn't, I just felt immense relief that the whole medieval, barbaric episode was finally over. Whoever says childbirth is a beautiful experience is lying – and it was probably a man who said it because no woman in her right mind would call what I've just experienced, beautiful.

As the entire, hideous event was about to come to a climax, Helen put a mirror in my hand and asked me if I wanted to watch the 'crowning'. I looked at her in confusion and she said, *don't you want to see the baby's head as it emerges?*

She was quite shocked when I said *no* but I don't care. Does anyone in full control of their faculties want to see something emerging from their body that's caused them indescribable pain and quite likely ripped them to shreds in the process?

I think not. I do think these midwives get a bit carried away with themselves sometimes. Just because they think giving birth is wonderful not everyone does and it's different for them, it's their *job* and they're not the one who's in agony.

Helen's dressing the baby in the pink Babygro and tiny hat that I brought with me, and I watch as she carefully wraps her in a blanket ready to give to me. I brace myself and know that I'm going to have to pretend, lie that I'm thrilled when in reality I feel nothing except exhaustion and all I really want is a cup of tea and a good sleep. All the way through this pregnancy I've been waiting for the maternal feelings to kick in but they haven't. Maybe I'm more like Mother than I thought I was. I'm going to have to lie just as I've always done – which is very sad but that's just the way it's going to be, I'm obviously not capable of love.

Although I'm not going to let that make me a bad mother. I'm still going to make a far better job of it than Mother did.

'There we go, mummy, a beautiful daughter.' Helen places the blanket wrapped bundle in my arms and I look down at her. Spiky, black hair pokes out from underneath the bonnet and her little face is red and screwed up and her hands are clenched into tight fists as if she's angry at being born. She suddenly opens her eyes and stares up at me and I swear she looks right into my eyes as if she knows who I am.

A strange feeling washes over me; it starts in the soles of my feet and it rushes up my body so quickly that I have trouble catching my breath. As it spreads over my chest I feel as if I've been physically punched. As I gaze into her eyes I realise that I'm crying, great gulping sobs that are making my body shudder.

'Oh Al, she's beautiful.' Doris coos.

She's more than beautiful, she's absolute perfection and she's mine. Is this love? Is this the feeling that everyone talks about and I've never experienced?

I don't know what it is or what to call it, but I do know that right at this moment the thought of anything bad happening to her is unbearable and that I would kill for her, in a heartbeat.

'She looks like you, Al.'

I gaze at her in wonder.

'What you gonna call her? You decided yet?'

I can't speak. I shake my head.

We've been talking of names for weeks but I still don't know and it doesn't matter right now; nothing matters. I might not know how to be a good mother but I can learn.

And even though I don't know how, I can learn because I *want* to. I want to do the very best that I possibly can. I know with absolute certainty that I'll never be like Mother. I'll never belittle my daughter or stop her from doing what she wants and she won't have a loveless, miserable upbringing like I did.

Although I will be *very* strict about one thing.

She's never, ever, going on a diet.

THE END

One last thing...

Thank you so much for reading this book. I really do appreciate it. If you have enjoyed this book I would be thrilled if you could leave a review or a star rating on Amazon or Goodreads. All of my books are available on Kindle Unlimited and you can view them on https://viewauthor.at/MarinaJohnson.

Printed in Great Britain
by Amazon

45309346R00169